CW01457274

Alice In Sunderland

For family and friends,

and the good people who read my books.

1.

Lady Henrietta Chesham was peering down her long, bony nose through the magnificent, mullioned dining room window of Chesham Manor. As her gaze took in the manor's sweeping parklike gardens and beautifully presented flowerbeds, a look of horrified disgust was spreading slowly across her face, as if someone had just placed something extremely nasty and foul-smelling beneath her nose.

'Humphrey!' she called out loudly to demand her husband's attention.

Lord Humphrey Chesham was hiding behind his morning broadsheet newspaper, trying to get up to speed with the latest goings on in the world, and pushing a fork around his breakfast plate of eggs benedict.

'Hmmm?' came his voice from behind the paper.

'There appears,' continued Lady Henrietta caustically, 'to be a troop of tracksuited troglodytes meandering through the grounds!'

Lord Humphrey sighed and slowly lowered his newspaper onto the dining room table. He fixed his wife with a look of sheer exasperation.

'You know very well that it's the annual open day today, Henrietta. And that troop, as you put it, happens to be the Great British public.'

'Does it, indeed?' snapped Lady Henrietta, unimpressed. 'Well, they'd better keep their Great British sticky fingers off the *Cytisus* this year.'

'My dear, what on earth are you talking about?'

'I swear to you, Humphrey, last year at least half a dozen of my best specimens went mysteriously missing. Well, I'm not having it. I'm going to have the groundsmen thoroughly frisk them all before they leave this time.'

Lord Chesham had just taken a sip of his tea and was now desperately trying not to choke on it.

'You'll do no such thing!' he spluttered. 'Without the open day our funding from British Heritage will be cut off! And we can ill afford that! You know as well as I how much this place costs to run. Besides, I'm quite sure no one is interested in stealing your Cystitis…'

'*Cytisus*, dear!' she corrected him. 'Lord only knows what you're thinking…'

'Well, whatever the bloody plants are called matters not a jot,' he told her angrily. 'The fact remains that we need the funding and, ergo, we need the open day. So, you'll just have to be nice to them, won't you?'

She scowled and gave him one of her most withering looks. But after thirty-odd years of marriage, Lord Chesham was quite immune to them. He resumed reading his paper and Lady Henrietta returned to the window to continue her spying.

*

Chesham Manor was, of course, the ancestral home of the Cheshams. It was an ancient, heavily beamed medieval manor house encompassed by an estate of several hundred hectares and was situated a few miles inland from the North Norfolk coast. As Humphrey was keen on pointing out at any opportune moment, it had even had a mention in the

4

Domesday Book. Although back then it was just a collection of farm buildings within a homestead.

The name of Chesham had begun to be associated with the manor since the early part of the Middle Ages, when an enterprising farmer by the name of Cuthbert Chesham had purchased the property and set about acquiring as much land as he could muster. Successive generations of Cheshams had continued the acquisition of land and had steadily added extensions to the existing farmhouse until it had become the huge and rambling manor house it was famously known as today.

At one point in its history, a moat had been dug out along the front boundary to protect against any potential invaders. A small drawbridge allowed access from one side to the other. The drawbridge was still in use as the main access to the entrance of the manor. Along with its housing it was a Grade One Listed special feature of the property.

Down the centuries the Cheshams had been a proud and noble family. They had endured almost a millennium by diligently sticking to the family motto:

Superstes Omni Pretio

(Survival At All Costs)

Sir Percival Chesham, a renowned medieval knight, had set the bar when he'd found himself up against the king's undefeated giant of a champion, Sir Cedric of Winchester, during a Royal Tournament in Norwich.

While Sir Cedric had been busy strutting his stuff and collecting favours from his many female admirers in the stands, Sir Percival had taken the opportunity to sneak up behind him and brutally stab him in the back, in a most unchivalrous manner. He'd then had the audacity to proclaim himself the undisputed victor of the tournament.

The king had not been best pleased with his dastardly behaviour, and poor Percival had been promptly imprisoned in Norwich dungeon, where he'd quickly come to a sticky end with the involvement of a red-hot poker, Edward II style.

And so, the standard had been set. And verily, over the centuries, when danger had reared its ugly head, and the Cheshams had needed to save their skins, they'd had no qualms about chucking their former closest friends and trusted allies under the nearest cart and horse. Or in more recent times, under a bus.

Lord Humphrey Chesham, likewise, had managed to endure in his chosen profession. And what's more, he'd managed it in a fashion conforming to the great family tradition. For the last forty years he'd been the Conservative Member of Parliament for his North Norfolk constituency. During that time, he'd been famous for presiding over a district where absolutely nothing had been changed or accomplished in any way, shape or form. And the vast majority of his constituents loved him for it.

But don't be fooled into thinking this was an easy task. Maintaining this level of inactivity for forty years had been no mean feat and had required a great deal of diplomacy, bribery, backstabbing, and good old-fashioned, two-faced deceit. Not to mention all the bare faced lying. All the hallmarks, in fact, of a successful politician.

Over the years, the liberal loony left and crazed eco warriors had tried to submit plans for various dreadful schemes in the district. Solar farms, wind turbines, bio-diesel facilities and recycling plants had all been proposed, but Humphrey had managed to thwart them all. Wind turbines – in his back yard? – not bloody likely. In his opinion, they looked like some sort of Martian invaders from *The War of The Worlds*. Nobody he knew of wanted those monstrosities blighting the landscape.

But a simple bribe at the right price to his insider at the planning department had ensured that all these proposals had surreptitiously found their way into the shredding machine.

An even trickier situation had been only a few years ago, when some blasted do-gooder had come up with the notion of a ghastly, garishly coloured children's playground to be installed on the village heath. Worryingly, it had garnered quite a lot of support from some of the locals who, it turned out, had a few kiddywinks of their own.

Well, he was having none of it. For a start, he'd be able to see it from the orangery window and he wasn't about to have his view ruined for the benefit of a few pizza-faced, pudgy youths. Besides which, if Henrietta had learned about the scheme, she would have had an absolute conniption. He'd had to come up with one of his more brilliant, underhanded plans.

He'd known from prior experience that the Health and Safety Executive could be a powerful ally in quashing any kind of activity designed to be carefree and fun. He had personally made an appointment with the manager of the department and commissioned him to carry out an extensive study of the playground proposal. Naturally, he had provided a hefty sweetener to the department to ensure the findings went his way. Which he'd later claimed as an administrative expense on his tax return.

The department had duly provided him with an eight-hundred-page document of utter fabrication, which could easily have won the Pulitzer Prize for Fiction. It was so mind numbingly dull and full of incomprehensible technical equations, graphs and drawings, that Humphrey knew for a fact that no one would actually read it. However, at his request, the department had also provided a summary of their findings, which was a far more palatable three pages in length. It went something like this:

1. **The Roundabout**. The study had found that if the roundabout was spun with sufficient RPMs, then any children, unless chained in place, would be flung off at a variety of velocities and trajectories, all resulting in calamitous injury, fractures and missing teeth.
2. **The Slide**. The study had found that if a child were to reach a certain speed* whilst descending the apparatus and inadvertently touched the sides of the plastic chute with a bare arm or leg, then at least half a yard of skin would be removed in the form of a friction burn.
   *(If anyone had bothered to read page 337 of the report, they would have discovered in the small print that this speed would need to be in excess of 50 mph.)
3. **The Swings**. The study had found that if a swing was swung any higher than an angle of 25 degrees, the chances of a child falling out of the chair were almost 100% certain, and with a high probability of injury. If both swings were swung simultaneously, then there would first be a painful, unavoidable mid-air collision. And then the children would fall out of the chairs, with an even higher probability of injury.
4. **The Seesaw**. The study had found that if a child at one end of the seesaw was significantly weightier than a child at the other, then the lighter child would likely be catapulted off the device, reaching a neck-breaking height before plummeting to the ground to land in a crumpled heap of bones, blood and guts.

To nail the point home, the department had also attached some particularly graphic and gruesome computer-generated pictures of all the potential injuries.

Humphrey had arranged a presentation in the village hall to explain the findings to the general public. In his concluding speech, he had advised the good folk of North Norfolk that unless the children in question were the offspring of a union between Indiana Jones and Lara Croft, then they would be unlikely to escape unharmed from the treacherous pitfalls and lethal traps that were contained in this insane project. The public had been horrified.

He'd then gone on to berate the proposer of the plan (who transpired to be a retired vicar named George) to be some sort of vile, child-maiming psychopath.

After suffering months of verbal and physical abuse from angry parents, the unfortunate George had subsequently had to sell up and emigrate to New Zealand.

For the Cheshams, however, it had all turned out to be most satisfactory.

*

Humphrey was now retired and, in thanks for his many years of loyal service, he had been awarded a peerage and, along with it, a seat in The House of Lords. A cushy job he'd been hankering after for a long time.

His former job of being the Conservative MP for his constituency in North Norfolk had been duly handed down to his daughter, Alice, and she'd proven most proficient in the last year since taking over. Humphrey was rightly very proud of her. She was the apple of his eye, and he doted on her. There was only one thing that worried him slightly about her, and it was that she wasn't particularly Chesham-like. She didn't appear to have inherited any of the famous family traits, at all. She wasn't cruel, unkind, heinous or despicable in any way, and as far as Humphrey was aware, she'd never plotted a devilishly diabolical scheme in her life. In fact, he had a sneaking suspicion that she may in fact be – dare he say it – quite *nice*.

A concern, however, that hadn't ever been raised about her younger brother, Alfie, who'd just stumbled sleepily through the doorway of the dining room looking like an extra from *Night Of The Living Dead*. His frizzy hair was sticking out in all directions, his eyes were half shut, his T-shirt was inside out, the flies on his trousers were undone and his socks had holes in the toes. A faint odour of stale alcohol was oozing from every one of his pores.

'And what time do you call this, Alfred?' asked Henrietta sternly, as she turned away from the window to face him. She always called him by his full Christian name when she was displeased with him.

'Erm, I dunno…around the crack of dawn?' Alfie suggested as he yawned loudly.

'Dawn was at a quarter past seven, young man,' Humphrey informed him. 'It is now five past ten.'

'Well, I did say *around* dawn, didn't I? Is there any brekkie left – I'm starving.'

'Carstairs cleared the breakfast plates away half an hour ago', said Henrietta, tutting at him.

Carstairs was Chesham Manor's long serving and loyal butler and had been in the family's employ for many a year.

'But, Mater, I'm starving,' he pleaded.

Henrietta rolled her eyes in annoyance as Humphrey shook his head in disbelief. But eventually she relented and rang the silver bell which was placed on the dining room table.

As they waited for Carstairs to reappear, Humphrey turned his attention to Alfie. He sometimes wondered how

10

he'd managed to produce such a useless reprobate. He really did worry about his son's ability to cut it in the big bad world. If anyone was a prime contender for a Darwin Award, it was Alfred. He had all the survival skills of a melancholic lemming. For instance, when he was a young boy learning to swim, he'd put on his armbands and launched himself enthusiastically into the deep end of the municipal swimming pool. Unfortunately, he'd neglected to inflate the armbands first, and thus sank like a stone, right to the bottom. He'd had to be rescued by the lifeguard. And as a teenager, along with his gormless friends, he'd had a go at glue sniffing and succeeded in supergluing his nostrils together. He'd almost asphyxiated before they'd managed to get him to A&E. And that had taken some explaining to the doctor on duty. Humphrey pondered what on earth he was to do with the boy.

'And what important plans do you have lined up for today, then?' Humphrey enquired of him.

Alfie shrugged. 'Well, I'll probably do some more work on the laptop,' he said.

'You mean you'll be wasting your time playing computer games?' accused Humphrey.

'But, Pater,' he cried, 'you don't understand. Super Mario won't get to the next level on his own...'

Humphrey sighed.

Henrietta took over. 'Getting to the next level of your silly game is not a viable career choice, Alfred,' she chastised him. 'And neither is staying out half the night with your debauched friends.'

'We're not debauched, Mater. We're the much-heralded Geronimo Club!'

'Much-heralded Geronimo Club!' scoffed Humphrey. 'And what exactly does that entail?'

'Well,' explained Alfie, pleased to have his parents' attention for once, 'essentially, what we do is…er.'

'Yes?' pressed Humphrey.

'We all meet up in our sports cars at a given, well-known location. And then – when everyone's ready – we all drive off as fast as we can and shout "Geronimo" as loudly as possible!'

'Then what?'

'Well…that's it, really.'

'You drive around shouting "Geronimo"?'

'Yeah, it's well cool. You should see the expressions on people's faces when they see us!'

'I can imagine,' said Humphrey.

Alfie, blissfully unaware of the sarcasm, was beaming with pride. It was short lived.

'Well, I don't want you shouting "Geronimo" any more,' Henrietta informed him.

The smile fell off Alfie's face. 'What? Why ever not?' he protested.

'It sounds common. And if you're going to go around making an exhibition of yourself, you can jolly well shout something more respectable.'

'But Mater…'

'No, not another word!' she scolded. 'I'll let you know when I think of something more appropriate. And if I hear "Geronimo" one more time, you're out of the will. Do you understand?'

'Yes, Mater,' he muttered dejectedly. He knew better than to argue with his mother once she'd made up her mind.

At that moment, Carstairs re-entered the dining room, complete with a tray bearing a hangover-busting plate of bacon, eggs and toast and a large mug of coffee. There was also some paracetamol and a glass of water.

Henrietta gave him an enquiring look.

'I had anticipated the ringing of the bell might be for the young master's reinvigoration, milady,' he said by way of explanation.

He smiled benevolently at Alfie as he placed the tray down in front of him. He was fond of the lad, even if he was a wayward chump.

Alfie smiled back happily and high-fived Carstairs' white gloved hand.

'You're the man, 'Stairs!' enthused Alfie, as he began tucking in to his bacon and eggs.

'Yes, sir.'

Carstairs turned his attention to Humphrey, and reaching into his jacket pocket, he produced a formal looking letter.

'This arrived with the morning mail, milord,' he said, handing the letter to Humphrey. 'It looked important so I thought I'd bring it up straight away.' Carstairs usually left the mail on the desk in Humphrey's study, but the letter bore the official seal of the government, which, of course, indicated a matter of some importance.

'Thank you, Carstairs,' smiled Humphrey, as he took the letter and ran his finger along the seam of the envelope. He pulled out the single sheet of top-quality paper and read it. It was very short. It simply requested his presence at an emergency meeting in Whitehall tomorrow at twelve noon. It was signed by The Chancellor of the Duchy of Lancaster, the most important cabinet member after the PM. *Must be damn important*, mused Humphrey. He placed the letter carefully in his pocket.

'Will that be all, sir?' asked Carstairs, who'd been politely waiting in the wings.

'Hmm?' murmured Humphrey, still lost in thought. 'Oh, yes, thank you, Carstairs. That will be all.'

'Milord,' chanted Carstairs and turned to leave.

'Oh, Carstairs?'

'Milord?'

'Did you happen to see Alice this morning?' enquired Humphrey.

Carstairs turned back to face Humphrey again. 'Yes, sir. Mistress Alice took her breakfast first thing this morning at seven o'clock sharp.'

'And then where did she dash off to?'

'She mentioned heading to the stables to attend to some equestrian chores, sir. I believe she intends to ride her horse over to the Polo Club later on this morning.'

'Oh? Whatever for?'

Carstairs was about to reply when he was interrupted by Alfie.

'Gosh, Pater,' he exclaimed. 'Even I know she's got a rally at the Polo Club today. In fact, me and the boys from the Geronimo Club are going over later to lend her some support.'

'I'm sure that will be a great comfort to her,' said Henrietta acerbically. 'And while we're on the subject, I've thought of a much more suitable name than Geronimo for you to proclaim to the world.'

14

She sidled over to where Alfie was sitting and leant over to whisper the new battle-cry in his ear. Alfie looked forlorn.

'Oh, Mater, you've got to be joking!' he moaned.

'I most certainly am not.'

'I won't do it!' he said determinedly.

'In that case, you'll be handing the car keys back.'

Alfie loved his sports car. He couldn't possibly part with it. She had him over a barrel, and he knew it.

'It's so unfair,' he complained.

'Life is unfair,' said Henrietta matter-of-factly. 'Get used to it.'

She then majestically turned on her heel and strode off outside and into the gardens to see if she could find some unsuspecting members of the public to persecute.

While Alfie slouched off to get showered, Humphrey went to his study to make some phone calls. Carstairs was left to tidy up the last of the breakfast dishes and take a quick break before starting preparations for lunch.

And so, another day commenced at Chesham Manor.

2.

The Honourable Alice Chesham MP had not been born with a silver spoon in her mouth. She'd been born with a diamond encrusted platinum spoon in her mouth. But this uber-privileged upbringing had not made her into an unpleasant person. She wasn't a diva, or arrogant, or superior or even bratty. Not at all. If you were to meet her, you might consider her to be the girl next door. Her feet were firmly planted on the ground.

Alice and Alfie had both started their education in life at the locally renowned Gressingham School. While the teaching staff had correctly surmised that Alfie had the neural capacity of your average jellyfish, Alice, however, had proven to be studious, academic and highly intelligent. She'd also excelled on the playing field, enjoying rounders and netball, while Alfie was more likely to be found smoking roll-ups behind the bike sheds. She'd finished Gressingham with straight 'A's in English, history and mathematics and gone on to study history and politics at Cambridge University. Alfie had finished with an 'U' in media studies and had gone on to fail his driving test seven times.

Alice had grown into an extremely attractive young woman, with sandy blonde hair which fell loosely over her shoulders, and dazzling azure blue eyes. She kept herself fit and strong and was the epitome of health and vigour. She had a love of the outdoors and a passion for horses and all things equestrian in particular. Her mother, who was also a keen rider, had introduced her to equestrian pursuits at a young age. Her mother still rode occasionally and kept a mare in the stables. Alice also had her own horse – a recent acquisition and her only extravagance – and he was a Thoroughbred colt named Jonty. Alice adored him and spent much of her time attending and grooming him.

It had just passed 10:30am and she'd finished mucking out the stables and grooming Jonty and was now in the process of fitting his saddle ready for riding. She wore a navy-blue polo top, cream jodhpurs and knee length tan leather riding boots. On her head she wore a traditional black velvet riding helmet. She had a political rally at the Polo Club at 11:30am and she wanted to impress them by arriving on horseback. The Polo Club adjoined the estate of Chesham Manor, so she was able to ride cross-country all the way there. She was going to take a long circuitous route of about five miles, so Jonty got some good exercise.

With one foot in the stirrup, she heaved herself up onto Jonty's saddle and they made their way out of the stable block. She took Jonty at a walking pace along the short drive and then brought him up to a trot once they'd reached the open fields. After a few minutes she increased the pace to a canter, and then, after another five minutes, when the horse's muscles had warmed up sufficiently, she pressed him into a full gallop. She relished the speed at which Jonty flew across the fields and was exhilarated when they bounded over a few small jumps. The wind was blowing through her hair and she was thoroughly enjoying the whole experience.

All too soon she could see the impressive playing fields, paddocks and stables of the Polo Club, and beyond them the lavish clubhouse itself. As she approached the perimeter of the club's grounds she pulled on Jonty's reins and with a shout of 'whoa!' she brought him to a halt next to a wooden access gate. She dismounted and then led him through the gate and onto a path that led towards the clubhouse. She mounted the horse again and slowly walked him along the path and into the car park where the entrance to the clubhouse was located. In the car park she noted a fleet of about eight sports cars all parked next to each other in formation. So far, she could see a Ferrari, a Porsche, a Lotus, a Maserati, a

17

Lamborghini, a Jaguar, and a Mercedes AMG. They'd been reversed into the parking spaces so that they were all ready to leave quickly. She knew they must belong to the Geronimo Club, and sure enough she now spotted Alfie's Aston Martin at the end of the row.

As she neared the entrance there was a sizeable crowd of Hooray Henrys, Ya-Yas, Champagne Charlies, Wags, Socialites and other entitled Hoi Polloi waiting to greet her. They'd all been enjoying the complimentary drinks and nibbles laid on by the Polo Club in her honour. The Geronimo Club were certainly making a dent on the buffet and helping themselves to handfuls of canapes.

As she dismounted again, one of the club's grooms appeared and took Jonty away to the stable block for some water and a rest. Alice went up the front steps of the clubhouse to polite applause and cries of 'Cheers!' from the waiting guests still quaffing their champagne. She raised her hand and waved at them, smiling graciously all the while. She made her way inside and into the main sumptuous lounge area, where she strode confidently up to the small podium that had been placed at the far end of the room, ready to use for her speech. As she went to stand behind the podium, she removed her riding helmet and shook out her long blonde hair behind her. She then turned to face her audience and gave them a broad smile.

She'd prepared her speech the previous day. She knew her constituents well, and she knew the speech would go down a storm. She was well aware of the issues that were important to them, and she made damn sure she championed their concerns. She started her speech close to home, promising to lobby for more rights for horse riders to use bridleways, byways and permissive tracks. All too often these pathways were obstructed or overgrown, making them impossible to ride through on horseback. She was going to use all her ministerial powers to ensure better access for equestrian pursuits. Naturally, this received a huge round of applause from the Polo Club members. Next, she expounded

18

on her plans to curb anti-social behaviour by banning hoodies and preventing teenagers from gathering in large intimidating groups. She was also going to crack down on littering, graffiti and fly tipping by introducing hefty fines and forcing those responsible into community service. Lastly, she was going to shake up the council and ensure that it introduced proper ecological and environmental policies for the protection of the countryside, woodland, marshland and the coastal waters of North Norfolk. No more would companies and industries get away with polluting the environment. Not on her watch.

This heartfelt pledge wound up the rally and was rewarded with a huge round of applause, cheering, hurrahing and whistles from her adoring crowd. A group of young men from the Polo Club hoisted her onto their shoulders and carried her jubilantly back outside as Alice held her arms above her head, punching the air in triumph.

To add to the air of excitement, a cacophony of revving sports car engines could be heard suddenly as the Geronimo Club were preparing their party piece. One by one, the sports cars left their parking spaces and following each other in turn, they proceeded to drive slowly up to where Alice was holding court. The Ferrari was the first to pass and, as the car reached her, the driver gave her a wave. The engine revved loudly.

'Geronimo!' the driver hollered at the top of his voice and sped off down the gravelled drive.

Next, the Porsche and the Lotus went by.

'Geronimo!'… 'Geronimo!' came the cries.

Then the Maserati, the Lamborghini, the Jaguar, and the Mercedes.

'Geronimo!' … 'Geronimo!' ... 'Geronimo!' … 'Geronimo!'

They all shot off down the drive to huge applause.

Finally, only the Aston Martin was left. As Alfie drew the sports car up beside his sister, he grinned at her and raised his eyebrows in what he hoped was a knowing fashion. He then gave her a determined wave. The engine revved madly. He drew a deep breath.

'Jeremy!' he shouted exuberantly at the top of his lungs.

With wheels spinning, he then flew off down the drive to join his companions. The crowd of onlookers were slightly confused and turned as one to look bemusedly at Alice, as if for explanation. In reply, Alice just shrugged and shook her head to indicate she was as puzzled as them by this strange new quixotic battle cry. Although she did have a sneaking suspicion her mother might have had something to do with it.

Henrietta had, in fact, chosen the name very carefully, as Jeremy Chesham was famed for mechanising the farming equipment of the estate during the industrial revolution.

The Polo Club men lowered Alice back down to the ground just as the stableboy returned to the car park with Jonty. She mounted up once again and, giving one last wave to the crowd, made her way back down the path, through the gate and back onto the open fields. In high spirits, she rode Jonty all the way back home at full gallop.

3.

Carstairs was behind the wheel of Lord Chesham's Bentley Mulsanne chauffeuring him to his meeting in Whitehall. Humphrey was in the back seat of the luxurious car catching up with some paperwork en route to London. He was a sucker for the old-fashioned cream leather and burr walnut veneer, and the Mulsanne's interior was fitted out in this traditioned style. They'd driven down through Swaffham and then cut across past Newmarket to the M11. From there it'd been motorway all the way to London, and they were now approaching Westminster and their ultimate destination in Whitehall close to the Houses of Parliament.

Carstairs was an excellent driver, as well as a talented chef and all-round exemplary butler. He was also one of Humphrey's most trusted advisors. They were almost best friends in as much as a 'master and servant' relationship can be. Carstairs possessed a most excellent analytical mind and often helped Humphrey with his policies, plans and occasional nefarious schemes. Humphrey very much valued Carstairs and he looked after him well.

Humphrey had instructed Carstairs to park up at his London club which was only a short walk from Whitehall. Carstairs was to wait in the club until Humphrey returned, and then they'd have luncheon in the club's dining room before heading back to Norfolk.

As Humphrey walked the short distance to the Chancellor of the Duchy of Lancaster's offices, where the meeting was to be held, he wondered for the umpteenth time what on earth the emergency was all about. He ascended the stone stairs at the front of the property and, on entering the front double doors, found himself in a tastefully decorated black and white tiled hallway. From here, he was promptly directed through to the private and secure wood-panelled boardroom situated at the rear of the building. Several lords, ladies, ministers and peers were already seated around the large rectangular oak board-table. He recognised all of them. They were the top brass of the government. Only the PM himself was missing. Presumably to protect him from any potential fallout from the emergency meeting. Humphrey took his seat and waited patiently with the others.

Presently, the door to the board room opened and the Chancellor of the Duchy of Lancaster swept into the room. He was carrying a dozen or so dossiers under his arm, and as he handed them out to the gathered ministers, his face was grim and stern. He looked a very troubled man.

Humphrey looked down at his copy of the dossier and noted the report was entitled:

'A Scandal in Belgravia'

Imprinted upon it were all the usual seals of secrecy and *For Your Eyes Only* warnings.

The Chancellor had finished handing out the dossiers and had returned to the head of the table. He placed his hands on the wooden surface and leaned forward to address everyone gathered for the meeting.

'Good morning, my lords, ladies and gentlemen,' he began. 'May I first of all thank you for your prompt responses to my letters and for attending today at such short notice.'

There was a general murmur of acknowledgement.

'I'm afraid I bear tidings of bad news,' he continued. 'As you have probably gathered, we have a very serious problem on our hands.'

'Well let's not beat about the bush, old bean,' said the Minister for Foreign Affairs. 'Let's have it out – warts and all.'

'Very well,' said the Chancellor, acquiescing. 'You are all, I'm sure, familiar with who holds the current post of Parliamentary Secretary to the Treasury?'

'You mean the Chief Whip?' queried the Minister for Justice. 'Well, of course. It's Sir Randall Panderyn, isn't it?'

There were many nods and mutterings of agreement from around the table. But then a cold laugh could be heard coming from somewhere down at the end.

'Sir Randall Panderyn!' scoffed the Minister for Defence, with a snort of derision. 'I went to Oxford with the blighter. Randy Pandy we used to call him! What's the old devil gone and done now, then?'

'Well, if you'd care to open your dossiers,' stated the Chancellor, 'you will find inside a set of photographs which will inform you, in no uncertain terms, precisely what he's been up to.'

Humphrey opened his dossier to the first page and found the pictures in question. As he stared at the images, his jaw nearly hit the floor. The first photograph clearly displayed the aforementioned Sir Randall chained with manacles to, what appeared to be, an iron ring on a dungeon wall. He was entirely naked except for a gag that was tied tightly into his mouth. For the sake of decency, his more intimate areas had been mercifully blurred out. Next to him was a leather clad dominatrix, wielding a hefty cat-o'-nine-tails, with which she had evidently been giving him a thorough spanking. The other photographs were in a similar vein, showing the sordid performance in a variety of angles and in the most excruciating detail.

'Good Lord!' exclaimed the Minister for State Affairs. 'Does he even know these images have been taken?'

'Yes, he does. In fact, as we speak, Sir Randall is being blackmailed for five hundred thousand pounds,' explained the Chancellor. 'If he doesn't pay, the lady in question is threatening to send the pictures to the tabloids. And we all know what that would mean. He urgently contacted me for assistance in the matter several days ago. And this is, of course, why I have summoned you all here.'

'Well, it's no good,' stated the Minister for the Environment. 'He'll have to lose the whip.'

'It would appear the lady has already taken care of that!' quipped the Minister for Justice.

There was an appreciative chuckle from around the room. The Chancellor was less amused.

'It's all very well making jokes,' he snapped, 'but how on earth can we provide a plausible explanation for what's going on in these pictures?'

Silence hung in the air for a good many seconds before one of the gathered ministers piped up.

'Here's a thought. Why don't we just say she's a motorcycle enthusiast?' suggested the Minister for State Affairs. 'I mean, she is wearing leathers.'

'Yes…but most motorcyclists,' pointed out the Chancellor, 'don't usually wear leathers with the backside cut out'.

'And I hardly think my department would approve *that* design,' added the Minister for Transport.

'Yes, I take your point,' conceded the Minister for State Affairs.

There was a further moment of reticence while they considered the problem. Eventually Humphrey spoke up.

'Who is this woman anyway? Do we have any idea?' he enquired.

'I've had Special Branch run an investigation on her,' replied the Chancellor. 'It's all in the dossier, but I can tell you that she's from Great Yarmouth, she's thirty-two years old and initially trained as a hairdresser. However, she soon discovered exotic dancing to be far more to her taste and a far more lucrative trade. She learned her profession as a stripper, lap-dancer and, subsequently, as a dominatrix, in a strip club called Lapland for many years, using the stage name Natasha Swish. Her real name is Yvonne Slade. She moved to London and started operating in Belgravia last year and has been making a small fortune entertaining her clients with a whole host of adult characters and fetishes. You'll find a copy of her pamphlet in the file. I suggest you take a look. She's quite the enterprising lady.'

Humphrey located the pamphlet in the dossier and turned his attention to it. On the front page was a seemingly innocent picture of her posing in a style of a fashion model. Inside the pamphlet, however, was an altogether different story. Humphrey could see she did indeed appear to have most genres fully catered for. In eye-watering detail. And at eye-watering prices. These included:

Natasha Swish, the headmistress with the cane of pain.

Juicy Lucy, the busty barmaid.

Queeny Todd, for the ultimate close shave.

Sister Nancy, the naughty nun.

Wanda Whiplash, the dungeon dominatrix.

Backdoor Betty, for cheeky fun.

Nurse Carla, guaranteed to raise your temperature.

April Showers, for enthusiasts of water sports.

25

And so, the list went on…

Lord Cecil Pemberton was reading the pamphlet with some difficulty. He was in his nineties and couldn't quite grasp what on earth was going on or why he was even here. He was looking forward to returning to his cosy rooms in The House of Lords but felt he ought to say something to justify his presence.

'I once had an aunty called Betty,' he ventured. 'She used to like the back door too.'

He detected a palpable silence falling on the room. As he looked up, he noticed that all eyes around the board-table were staring at him. He felt they were waiting for further elaboration.

'When she came to visit,' he added, 'she had a key for the back door.'

'Thank God for that,' muttered the Chancellor, who'd been wondering where this latest revelation was headed.

Humphrey intervened again as he desperately tried to restore some common sense to the proceedings.

'But where is this Yvonne Slade now?' he asked.

'Done a bunk,' came the Chancellor's short reply. 'Disappeared into the ether and left us only with the blackmail note and details of her Swiss bank account.'

The Right Honourable Minister for Business and Trade took to his feet and, waving the dossier angrily in his right hand, began a tirade.

'This is an absolute travesty!' he proclaimed. 'I'm old enough to remember the Profumo Affair, but this makes that scandal look like a Mills and Boon romance! It's just the sort of sleaze that will bring down the government! Disgraceful!'

He sat down again looking distraught before shuffling the dossier papers into a neat pile and surreptitiously secreting them into his briefcase for a more thorough perusal later on.

'It's all very well shouting and bawling,' said the Chancellor, 'but we need to act. And fast. We need solutions – not lectures!'

The Minister for Justice looked pensive for a moment, but then made up her mind as to what she thought they must do.

'We've no choice but to pay her,' she stated. 'The risk of this getting to the press is just too great.'

'Agreed,' concurred the Minister for State Affairs. 'But Sir Panderyn will have to go – no two ways about it.'

'And the bloody fool can pay the blackmailer out of his own pocket. I don't see why we should use party funds,' added the Minister for Foreign Affairs.

There was a murmur of general assent.

'And to throw the hounds off the scent, I recommend we replace him with someone reliably dull and dutiful,' suggested the Minister for Justice.

The Chancellor nodded his head enthusiastically.

'I know just the fellow,' he said. 'Giles Wight – dull as ditchwater – he's our candidate up in Sunderland. He's not making any progress up there either, so no one would miss him.'

'Good idea,' chipped in the Minister for State Affairs.

'But who would then take over his candidacy?' questioned Humphrey.

27

The Chancellor considered the issue for a moment before replying.

'Your girl's doing well in your old constituency, isn't she?'

'Alice? Yes, she very competent.'

'Do you think she'd relish the challenge?'

'Taking on Sunderland, you mean?

'I do,' said the Chancellor seriously. 'We really do need a go-getter to work some magic up there. I think Alice might be just the ticket. What do you think, old friend? You'd really be helping us out.'

'Well, I'd have to ask her,' said Humphrey, 'but she always did like an ambitious endeavour.'

'Excellent!' exclaimed the Chancellor. 'And young Alfred, I'm sure, can take over things in Norfolk…'

'Alfred?' queried the Minister for the Environment. 'But isn't he a complete and utter idio…er…idiosyncratic type?'

Humphrey gave him a stern look.

'I'm sure Lord Chesham is well aware of his son's strengths and weaknesses,' cut in the Chancellor diplomatically. 'And so, I think our work here is done. I'll get the necessary wheels in motion. Well done everyone and my thanks again!'

'Hmph?' called out Lord Pemberton, jolting awake from a snooze. 'Is it lunchtime?'

As a matter of fact, it was.

The meeting broke up and the ministers drifted off to attend to their own affairs. Humphrey hurried back to his club, where he met up with Carstairs. Over a long luncheon, the two men discussed all the events that had taken place and devised a detailed plan for the best way forward.

4.

On the return trip to Norfolk, Humphrey had telephoned the manor and spoken with Henrietta. He'd asked her to arrange a household meeting and to ensure both Alice and Alfred were in attendance. Everyone was to gather in the dining room at eight o'clock sharp. Humphrey had wanted Carstairs there too, so he'd given him the night off from his duties. Covering in his place, Alice had made a simple dinner of cold cuts and salad for herself and her mother and brother, which they'd eaten round the kitchen table.

Just before eight o'clock they made their way into the dining room, where Humphrey and Carstairs were waiting for them. Humphrey filled them in on all the details of what had transpired at his meeting in London. Alfie had not been able to stop himself from giggling at Sir Randall's escapades. But when it came to light about Alfie's new impending career, with all the formality and responsibility it entailed, the smirk had soon fallen off his face.

'Pater,' he implored. 'I'm not ready. I can't be MP for North Norfolk. I don't have the experience. I'm only twenty-two years old.'

'And a complete clot,' added Henrietta.

'Exactly!' Alfie concurred, nodding vigorously, and agreeing with his mother for once.

Humphrey placed a hand on Alfred's shoulder and looked him squarely in the eye.

'Your renowned ancestor, Jeremy Chesham, was only nineteen when he took over the reins and revolutionised farming on the estate,' he told him. 'And Alice was only a year older than you when she took over.'

'That's right, Alfie,' said Alice, trying to boost his morale. 'You'll be just fine. You'll see.'

'But I'm not like you,' he moaned. 'You're clever and organised, and I'm…hopeless….'

A soft clearing of a throat nearby interrupted the discussion and everyone's attention turned towards the butler.

'If I may interject, My Lord,' intoned Carstairs. 'With your permission, I'd like to take young Alfred under my wing for a week. I believe he would benefit from my tutelage in the ways of comporting oneself with confidence and respectability.'

'An excellent idea,' beamed Humphrey happily. 'I'm sure you can work your magic on him.'

Alfie didn't look too sure. Neither did Henrietta, who had severe doubts if even the highly competent Carstairs could instil a Pygmalion effect on him. But Alice was nodding as enthusiastically as her father. Presently Humphrey turned his attention to his daughter.

'And, my dear girl, what have you to say about the opportunity of taking on Sunderland?'

Alice looked seriously at her parents and said in earnest, 'I'm honoured that The Chancellor of the Duchy of Lancaster has faith in my abilities. I'd relish the chance of getting my teeth into real politics. No offence, Pater, but there's nothing too onerous to deal with in these parts. You've had it all sewn up for years and I've just followed suit.'

'You're too modest, Alice,' chided Henrietta gently. 'You've introduced a whole raft of policies into the area that your father has ignored for years.'

Humphrey raised an eyebrow in annoyance, 'Such as?' he enquired testily.

'I'm referring to her environmental reforms, Humphrey,' she replied. 'You've got to admit you're clueless in that regard. If you recall, you thought there was a hole in the *N-Zone* for years!'

'Yes, well...,' he responded guiltily, 'I have to admit Alice has a better grasp of those particular issues than I.'

Henrietta smiled smugly.

'But let's return to the task in hand, shall we?' he continued. 'I propose we arrange a formal drinks party here at the manor. Shall we say in a week's time? So that we can ring the changes with all those involved. I'm inviting the Chancellor, Sir Randall Panderyn and Giles Wight to attend so we can all cordially exchange duties in a calm manner. And don't forget that what occurred to Sir Randall is completely confidential. It is an official state secret. No one is to mention it! Understand?'

They all nodded in acknowledgement.

'Excellent,' concluded Humphrey. 'Well, it's been a long day. Let's get ourselves turned in. We've got a busy week ahead.'

Alice and Alfie bade their mother and father goodnight, gave their blessings to Carstairs and headed off upstairs. Humphrey and Henrietta followed close behind while Carstairs went off to his own annex of rooms located at the rear of the manor.

*

During the following week Humphrey was going to make sure the changes were being implemented with no objections, and with the absolute minimum of publicity. He'd essentially taken over as Chief Whip from the now redundant Sir Randall. He'd been on the phone many times with The Chancellor, keeping him informed of progress. In order not to arouse suspicion as to Sir Panderyn's hasty disappearance from the public eye, it had been decided that the best course of action was to have him made a peer. He could then be safely buried with all the other old fossils on the backbenches of The House of Lords. Sir Randall had been thrilled at the news as, to his mind, this meant he could now carry on his sordid lifestyle in relative obscurity. The fact that this little venture had cost him half a million pounds was a minor inconvenience. The Panderyn family fortune was currently valued in excess of three hundred million pounds.

Alice had been busy tidying up her affairs ready for her transfer to Sunderland. Giles Wight had been in touch to enquire if Alice wished to continue the services of his PA in Sunderland, a one Barry Higgins, a man whom Giles heartily recommended. Alice had said she'd be delighted. Giles was going to bring Barry along to the drinks party so she could meet him in person. Alice had also been compiling extensive notes to pass along to Alfie to help him settle into his new post.

Henrietta had been entrusted to take care of Jonty. She and Alice had met most mornings in the stable block, where Alice had instructed her mother on Jonty's likes, dislikes and general foibles. Henrietta had assured her she had nothing to worry about – and that she was more than capable of looking after a flighty Thoroughbred!

On another note, Henrietta had received a request from her younger sister, Baroness Harriet Billingbrooke, if it would be propitious that she could also attend the drinks party. Henrietta and Harriet had been thick as thieves whilst growing up. They'd since gone their separate ways but always kept in touch. Given their parents had christened them with names starting with the same letter, when Henrietta had married Humphrey, she'd decided to continue the tradition and named their own children likewise. Hence Alice and Alfred. She'd thought it rather a hoot.

The Baroness was very proud of her niece and wanted to wish her all the best before she set off for the deepest, darkest reaches of the North East. Alice, in turn, was extremely fond of her Aunt Harri, even if she was as mad as a teapot. Harriet had been widowed a few years ago when her husband, Baron Eric Billingbrooke, had suffered a tragic and unexpected heart attack. She'd been the sole heir of his estate and fortune. Harriet had always been an eccentric lady but since her husband's passing, she'd developed a penchant for dressing in a rather manly fashion. She nearly always wore a three-piece trouser suit and was never without her umbrella. Alice also knew she was one of the few people who could unsettle her mother, which endeared Aunt Harri to her all the more. At any rate, Alice informed Henrietta that she'd be most welcome to attend.

Carstairs had taken Alfie into Norwich, where they'd spent the afternoon at Jarrold's department store to have Alfie fitted out with some smart new attire. They'd come home with several impeccably cut suits, half a dozen shirts and ties, and some fine black leather shoes. Carstairs had presented Alfie to the family neatly suited and booted in his new regalia. However, with his crazily unkempt hair and slouching demeanour he still only managed to resemble a well-dressed tramp. But Carstairs persevered. The following day Alfie was deposited at the barber's in Holt, where his wayward locks were tamed into something approaching a sensible haircut. The barber had also taken the opportunity to shave all the bumfluff from Alfie's top lip and chin with a straight razor, much to Alfie's dismay. When he was presented to the family again, this time they had to admit he actually looked fairly normal. Carstairs now just needed to work on the slouching and then begin some voice coaching, but he was confident of turning Alfred from a scruffy frog into a charming prince by the end of the week.

*

The week flew by and the day of the drinks party was soon upon them. That evening, the Cheshams were gathered in the manor's baronial drawing room, dressed to the nines and ready to receive their guests. Carstairs was hovering by the main entrance doors of the drawing room with a tray full of champagne flutes.

The first guest to arrive was the Baroness. She bowled into the room dressed in her habitual masculine three-piece suit. She helped herself to a glass as she swept past Carstairs, and then cordially greeted Henrietta and Humphrey. She gave Alice a warm smile and a peck on the cheek and congratulated her on her new undertaking. Alice beamed happily back at her.

'Good evening, Baroness,' said a handsome well-heeled man, as he took her gloved hand and gently pressed it to his lips with a small bow. The Baroness was rather taken aback.

'Who the bloody hell are you?' she asked rather abruptly.

The young man lifted his head slightly and gave her a cheeky grin.

'It's me, Aunt Harri. Alfie!'

The Baroness produced a monocle from her jacket pocket, placed it in her right eye and scrutinised the young fellow carefully.

'Well, bugger me sideways!' she proclaimed. 'So, it is! I barely recognised you, my boy. Don't you look the part!'

Carstairs, serving Humphrey and Henrietta with drinks nearby, allowed himself a rare smile.

The Chancellor was the next to arrive, closely followed by Giles Wight and Barry Higgins. Barry was fidgeting around awkwardly in his dinner jacket and bow tie. He clearly was not used to being dressed quite so formally. Many other guests were pouring in now. Local dignitaries, landed gentry, members of the clergy, and other important people of note were among the many guests.

Giles made a beeline for Alice, dragging Barry behind him. He was desperate to introduce himself and Barry to his new successor. As they approached, Giles reached out a hand to Alice which she took and gave a gentle shake.

'I'm delighted to meet you, Alice,' he said timidly. He was slightly in awe of the surroundings and was a little star struck to meet the new rising star in the Tory party. And no one had told him how stunningly attractive she was, which added further to his general apprehension.

'Nice to meet you too, Giles,' she smiled candidly. 'Sorry about all this highfalutin' pomp and ceremony. Not really my thing…but my parents do enjoy "putting on the Ritz" whenever they get an excuse.'

Giles breathed a sigh of relief to discover Alice was so easy to talk to. He'd been expecting her to have a plum in her mouth. 'That's okay,' he replied. 'It's a lovely place you have here.'

He shuddered inwardly at making such a corny line but she didn't seem to have noticed, or at least, was pretending not to. He hurried on.

36

'May I introduce my colleague?' he continued, indicating Barry, who was fiddling with his collar. 'Mr Higgins.'

Alice offered her hand. 'Lovely to meet you, Mr Higgins.'

Barry gave her a big friendly smile and grasped her hand warmly, giving her a shake that nearly caused her to spill her drink.

'How pet,' he garbled, 'ees offa canny a met yer tee.'

Alice stared at him blankly in confusion. 'Sorry,' she stated, 'it's a bit loud in here. I didn't quite catch that…'

'Nay wurrees,' he said, 'ah wus jus gan ta see worra reet belta o' a hoose ye han 'ere.'

Alice continued to stare blankly. She was a bit confused. She hadn't realised that Barry wasn't English. She couldn't quite place the language, but she was pretty sure the dialect was Scandinavian. Norwegian perhaps.

'Are you enjoying your trip?' she tried again.

'Ooh aye,' came the reply, 'we cam doon thur a reet bonnee toon on wor waa uver.'

'And will you be returning to Oslo soon?' she enquired in desperation.

'Sorree?' said Barry, getting confused himself now.

Giles' shoulders were shaking and Alice noticed that tears of laughter were coming down his cheeks. As he wiped the tears away, he addressed Alice.

'Don't worry, you'll get used to the accent before long.'

'Accent?' asked Alice.

'Barry is as English as you and me,' explained Giles. 'He's from Tyneside, born and bred. And his accent is pure Geordie.'

Realisation dawned on Alice. She was a little embarrassed.

'I'm so sorry, Barry,' she apologised. 'I didn't mean any offence.'

'Nun teekin, lassee,' smiled Barry genially. 'I nerr a soond a bit odd ta yee. Nay wurrees.'

'Nay wurrees,' said Alice, smiling back, and making Barry chuckle.

At that moment, the conversation was interrupted by Carstairs announcing the tardy arrival of Sir Randall Panderyn, whose chauffeur-driven Rolls had just pulled up outside. He entered the room as if he were minor royalty, beaming broadly and waving his hand graciously at the gathered guests. He was a short man, slightly overweight and with a discernible pot-belly. His face had the complexion of a heavy drinker, with ruddy cheeks, sallow eyes and a blotchy red nose. What was left of his hair was dyed dark brown and was arranged in an extremely unconvincing comb-over to hide his balding scalp. He'd clearly been drinking beforehand and he had a pronounced wobble as he swayed his way around the drawing room greeting the gathered guests. This didn't, of course, discourage him from downing several more glasses of champagne as he continued to saunter around. Eventually he made his way over to the far side of the room where Alice was standing, and sidled up beside her, patently leering at her well-dressed figure.

'Now haven't you grown up to be a fine-looking filly!' he pronounced loudly as he pinched her bottom lustily. The Right Honourable Sir Panderyn was most definitely The Wrong Dishonourable Sir Panderyn.

Alice could scarcely believe the sheer brazen audacity of the man and the blood boiled in her veins.

'I'm not a bloody horse, you know!' she retorted angrily. 'And I'll thank you to keep your hands to yourself.'

The angry outburst had not gone unnoticed. Humphrey caught her eye and his expression implored her not to make a scene. Henrietta and Harriet were watching her with interest.

'Merely giving you a compliment,' smarmed Sir Randall, who'd not taken kindly to the rebuke. 'No need to get excited.'

Alice felt her skin crawl, yet she managed, with great restraint, to keep her anger under control. But now, she resolved determinedly, she was going to teach the horrid little creep a damn good lesson.

Changing tack, she fixed a fake smile on her lips and turned to face Sir Randall.

'Forgive me,' she breathed huskily. 'I can be such a naughty girl.'

Sir Randall's eyes lit up. Alice continued to smile sweetly.

'And my heartfelt congratulations on being made a peer, your Lordship,' she continued.

'Why, thank you, my dear,' he said, clearly enjoying Alice's softer demeanour. 'And I must congratulate you too. Tell me, how do you think you'll fare up in Sunderland?'

Many of the guests had halted their own conversations and were now listening intently to what Alice and Sir Randall were discussing. Humphrey was relieved to see that they were being amicable.

'Oh, I'm not sure yet,' she replied demurely, 'but I'll certainly be giving it a fair *crack of the whip*!'

Sir Randall gave an involuntary flinch at the mention of a whip. *Does she know about my little faux pas?* he wondered. But then he reasoned he was being too sensitive and continued the conversation. More and more guests were taking an interest in the discussion.

'Well, you'll certainly have your work cut out for you,' he said.

'Oh yes, but I'll soon have things *whipped into shape.*'

A bead of sweat broke out on Sir Randall's brow. There it was again. Surely no coincidence this time. And he was sure he'd noticed a few smirks on the faces of the guests. He pressed on regardless.

'Oh, I agree. You'll really need to motivate your staff, won't you?' he stammered uncertainly.

'Absolutely!' exclaimed Alice as loudly as she could. 'I'll really need to *get cracking*! And then, once everything's been *thrashed out*, with *lashings* of effort, I'll really be able to *whip things up*!'

This time there were snorts of uncontrollable snickering from those in the know. A panicked Sir Randall looked feverishly round the room and, on seeing the laughing faces, realised to his horror that she had totally humiliated him. Red faced, he ran for the door amidst gales of mocking laughter.

Henrietta and Harriet were glowing with pride. Carstairs was struggling to keep the smirk off his face. Alfie was doubled up. Giles and Barry were grinning like Cheshire cats. Even Humphrey had to admit she'd conducted herself admirably.

'Well done, young lady,' congratulated the Chancellor, who'd been truly impressed. 'You certainly stood up for yourself and put Randy Pandy in his place!'

Alice graciously and modestly accepted the praise. She was relieved that he didn't seem cross with her.

The Chancellor wasn't cross. He was delighted. Any doubts he'd had in his mind about her being the right choice for the job had just evaporated.

'I propose a toast,' proclaimed the Chancellor cheerily, lifting his glass. 'To Alice!'

'To Alice!' chorused the room.

5.

Sunderland Docks Working Men's Club, locally known as 'The Dockers', was not a building that could be described as pleasing to the eye. It had been erected in the 1960s when constructing dull, basic, concrete blocks was considered by some to be architecturally groundbreaking. True to form, The Dockers was a flat roofed, butt-ugly, grey, square, squat blob of a building, completely devoid of any kind of imagination, character or flair whatsoever. In a nutshell, it had all the aesthetic qualities of a breeze block.

To be fair though, the whole enterprise had been conceived on a shoestring budget, and back in the day, in post war Britain, that meant only one thing: good old concrete. On the inside, however, it did have all the necessary equipment required to provide a venue for entertaining working men. Namely, it had a barroom, complete with some tables and chairs. And along one wall was a small stage, where anyone suicidal enough to attempt to entertain the workers could perform their act, before being pulverised and thrown into the street.

Also, in accordance with the first-class facilities, situated in the entrance hall were doors to ladies' and gents' lavatories. At some point in its history, a thoughtful youth had taken the time to scrawl a pair of breasts on the door to the Ladies, and a cock and balls on the door to the Gents. Presumably for the benefit of any visiting foreigners struggling to grasp the English language.

The club was situated within walking distance of the docks in a residential area just west of the River Wear. The neighbourhood was rough and run down and the inhabitants were tough looking people. Even the water was hard in this part of town.

The Labour MP for the area, Alan Bailey, had just driven his reliable old Volvo into the car park, and was parking up. He was here to attend his monthly meeting with the Sunderland Dock Workers Union boss, 'Red' Len Finch, and was running a few minutes behind schedule. Alan knew Len was a stickler for time keeping. He rushed through the front door, clutching his paperwork in an untidy mess, and hurried into the main bar area, a little out of breath.

'You're late,' came the monotone voice of Len Finch, who was sat waiting at one of the tables with his paperwork all neatly laid out in front of him. 'Timeliness is next to godliness, brother.'

'Red' Len had a strange way of talking. He referred to everyone as his brother or sister, and spoke in an old-fashioned manner, as if he were a character from a Victorian novel. It irritated the crap out of Alan, but he had to go along with it. He knew only too well that the power and the influence of the unions were critical to his political party's success, and he wasn't about to rock the boat. But try as he might to like the fellow, he found Mr Finch to be a fundamentally difficult, petty and unlikeable character.

'Sorry, Len, but my last meeting overran a little,' replied Alan. 'I came as quickly as I could.'

Len sucked in his cheeks and raised his eyes. 'I should think better organisation is the key, brother. Not excuses.'

Alan stared obstinately back at him and didn't reply. There was an awkward silence for a few moments.

'No matter,' continued Len. 'Let us begin, shall we?'

'By all means,' replied Alan.

Len picked up the top sheets of paper in front of him and studied them for a few seconds. 'I see our adversaries in the Tory party have been busy making changes,' he stated.

'Yes, indeed,' responded Alan. 'That news came as quite a surprise.'

Alan had actually had a very affable working relationship with Giles Wight. The two men had great respect for one another despite being at different ends of the political spectrum. When he'd heard the news that Giles was leaving, he'd rung him to ask if all was well. Obviously, Giles had been unable to tell Alan the real reason for the changes, but he'd thanked him for his concern and told him that it was just a routine re-shuffle that Conservative head office had decreed.

'And I see that his replacement will be a female,' Len remarked.

What a strange way of putting it, thought Alan. 'Yes, a young lady named Alice Chesham. Coming up from Norfolk, I believe.'

Len's eyes narrowed. 'She's the daughter of Lord Humphrey Chesham, an extremely wealthy and opulent landowner,' he said with no small hint of malice.

'I believe so,' said Alan, matter-of-factly.

'Just the type of person that will oppress and exploit the poor and working classes. Her presence here will be most unwelcome,' Len proclaimed with passion.

'Hang on a minute!' countered Alan. 'We don't even know her. I wouldn't go that far.'

Len scrutinised Alan unfavourably from over the top of his papers. He ran his fingers through his greying, Brylcreemed hair and then pretended to inspect his fingernails.

'Speaking as head of this union, you are aware of my political convictions, are you not?' he said testily.

'Well, of course, but…'

'I believe in socialism. I must defeat inequality and privilege wherever I see it. I'm a Marxist at heart, Alan. You have heard of Karl Marx, I presume?'

Alan was more than a little peeved at Len's condescending question. He decided to knock him off his high horse.

'Of course, I have,' retorted Alan. 'But he's not as funny as his brothers.'

The attempt to lighten the mood with a little witticism fell rather flat. Unfortunately, Mr Finch's sense of humour was sadly lacking in two vital components. Namely, sense, and humour.

Len just stared impassively at him. Alan was sure he saw a tumbleweed roll across the floor just behind him.

'It is not a laughing matter, brother,' said Len acidly.

'Clearly,' sighed Alan. 'Shall we move on to the next agenda, then?

'As you wish,' said Len coldly.

They both shuffled through their papers until they had the next item on the agenda.

'This item regards the takeover of Sunderland docks by the American company Lone Star Freight,' stated Alan seriously.

'And what have you to say about this turn of events, brother?' enquired Len suspiciously.

'As we all know,' replied Alan, 'Sunderland docks has been on its knees for years. What they really need is an

45

injection of new money and ideas. I believe the owner of Lone Star Freight intends to do just that.'

'The owner is none other than Texan billionaire Senator Earl Sanderson III,' Len informed him.

'Yes, I know,' said Alan. 'I think he'll be good news.'

'I have to disagree, brother,' came Len's response.

Here we go, thought Alan. Some might say Len Finch was a well-balanced man. In as much as he had a chip on *both* shoulders.

'And why's that?' queried Alan, as if he didn't know.

'He's a western capitalist of the worst kind! He cares not for the working man. He's a bombastic megalomaniac with more money than any human has a right to possess!'

'But he wants to send some of that money over here!' Alan pointed out.

'I cannot allow monetary gain to outweigh my duty of care to my comrades!' said Len ardently. 'I couldn't conscience it!'

'But without the investment the docks will be forced to close! Then what will happen to your comrades?' Alan implored him to see reason.

'The workings of capitalist industry is not my concern,' declared Len. 'I will not stand by and see my comrades exploited. In the circumstances I have no alternative but to call a strike!'

'A strike!' wailed Alan. 'Are you mad?'

'My mind is made up, brother,' Len decreed hotly. 'First thing in the morning – all work at the docks will cease!'

Alan stared at him incredulously. 'You can't be serious. You'll ruin us!'

46

'I'm deadly serious, Mr Bailey,' said Len rising to his feet. 'And now if you'll excuse me, I think our work here is at a close.'

'Red' Len gathered his papers together and marched purposefully out of the club, leaving Alan sitting at the table in dejection.

What the hell is going to happen now? wondered Alan. He had a horrible feeling the shit was about to hit the fan.

6.

'*Can I do it?*' Senator Sanderson hollered his catchphrase at the huge boisterous crowd gathered for his rally in the Port of Galveston, Texas.

'*Can you do it? Can you do it?*' roared the crowd in response.

'*Hell yeah!*' he shouted back to them at the top of his voice.

As the crowd whooped and whistled, he drew his custom-made Colt 45 revolver from its holster and fired several shots into the air, in what was now his trademark celebration after the finale of one his speeches.

'*Yee haa!*' he bawled loudly. The crowd responded wildly in kind.

Everything about Senator Earl Sanderson III was *big*. He was a heavily built man, stood six feet two inches tall, had broad shoulders, a barrel of a chest, and legs like tree trunks. In his youth, he'd been quite a football player, playing quarterback for his college team in Houston. Now aged in his mid-fifties, he'd gained some pounds around his waist but still held a respectable figure. He always dressed smartly in a Texan style business suit and wore a huge Stetson which he never publicly removed from his head. This was largely due to the fact that he wore a toupee to cover his rapidly receding hairline. And you didn't have to be Sherlock Holmes to spot that the toupee was an ever so slightly darker shade of gingery blond than Earl's natural hair colour. It made him look slightly ridiculous but no one in his close circle had had the guts to tell him. His necktie was a bolo or bootlace style, with metal tipped aiguillettes and a silver decorative clasp in the shape of a star to match his company logo. On his feet he wore brown leather cowboy boots with fancy decorative piping running up the sides. On the back of his boots were small imitation brass spurs which made a faint *ching* sound every time he took a step.

With dazzling bleached white teeth, the senator flashed his perfect gameshow host smile one last time and then turned to make his way off the stage. As he did so he signalled to a gigantic hulk of a man, dressed all in black, who was standing solidly by the nearby exit.

The huge man had black slicked-back hair, wore dark sunglasses and had a wire dangling from an earpiece inserted in his left ear. His massive right hand raised to touch the earpiece and he gave an inaudible instruction into a microphone concealed in the cuff of his jacket sleeve.

*

The man's name was Franco Gambini, and a more dangerous, menacing and ruthless killing machine you would be hard pressed to find. As a youth, Franco had been raised in a down and out area of Los Angeles by a violent, loud and fiery Italian American family. When his parents had acrimoniously split, neither had wanted to care for Franco and he'd been dumped in a Catholic orphanage at the tender age of eight. He'd soon had his fill of the nuns' strict regime and had disappeared one night preferring to live rough on the streets. He rapidly found himself in bad company and subsequently hung out for many years running with the gangs of Los Angeles, causing carnage wherever he went. But it wasn't long before his lethal talents were noted by a small-time mobster, Don Romano, who recruited him as one of his hitmen. Franco was only nineteen but soon started to make

49

some serious money dealing out pain, death and destruction on the mobster's many enemies. One such hit was to 'take care' of the rising businessman and statesman, Earl Sanderson III, who was trying to shut down one of the Don's drug smuggling operations in the port of Texas City.

Franco was to be paid $20,000 for the hit. Don Romano had supplied him with Earl's address, Starlight Ranch, located in the prairie lands south of Houston. In the dead of night, Franco had entered the grounds of the sprawling ranch, knocked out the guard stationed at the main gate, and then cut the power to the ranch's security systems. He easily broke into the main house and within a matter of minutes had found the upstairs master bedroom suite. Correctly surmising that this would be where he'd find his target, he approached the super king size bed containing the sleeping form of Earl, drew his silenced pistol and held it gently against Earl's temple. The sound of the hammer being cocked woke Earl from his slumber.

'What in the name of goddamn Methuselah is going on?' demanded Earl, still half asleep.

'You're a dead man,' replied Franco venomously, 'courtesy of Don Romano.'

Earl sat up in bed but understanding did not yet register in his mind.

'Don who?' he queried, confused. 'I ain't never heard of no Don Romano.'

'He's the man whose smuggling racket you've been messing with,' Franco told him. Franco liked his victims to know exactly why they were being bumped off. It was only common courtesy. 'And he's the man going to be paying me twenty grand to see you off, cowboy.'

Understanding finally dawned on Earl. But, true to form, he was far more concerned with the monetary side of things than his own life.

'Twenty grand?' he said incredulously. 'That's all I'm worth to this son of a bitch?'

'Seems so,' smirked Franco, about to pull the trigger. 'Any last words?'

'One hundred grand,' said Earl vehemently.

'What?'

'Twenty grand is chickenfeed, boy. An insult. I tell you what,' said Earl getting his business mind in gear. 'I'll pay you one hundred grand *not* to kill me. How's that sound?'

'And I suppose you have one hundred grand just lying around, huh?'

'Not lying around, boy. I ain't crazy. But I got it in the safe. Just over yonder,' he said indicating an oil painting hanging opposite the bed.

The gun was removed from his temple but stayed aimed squarely on him.

'Show me,' said Franco suspiciously. 'And no funny business. I can shoot you just as easily from here.'

Earl nodded, then eased himself out of bed and padded over to the painting. He lifted it off the wall to reveal a safe fixed into the wall behind it. He punched a code into the electronic keypad, and with a whirring click the locking bar slid back and the safe opened. Inside, the safe was stuffed full with bundles of bank notes. Earl picked up one of the wads and flicked through it to show Franco that each note was a hundred-dollar bill.

'Each one has fifty notes,' Earl explained. 'So, each wad is worth five grand.'

'There's more than twenty wads in there,' Franco pointed out.

'Hot diggity! Now we had a deal, boy,' lamented Earl. 'Don't tell me you're going to rob me too! Don't you have no morals?'

Franco raised an eyebrow. 'Is that a trick question?' he asked wryly.

Earl raised his hands in surrender.

'Okay, boy, you got me!' he admitted. 'There's two hundred grand in there. You take it all. But what I ask in return is that you go back to this Don Romano, and you reverse the hit. And just before you take him out, you tell him from me that before he takes on Earl Sanderson III, he's gonna need some deeper pockets. *Hell yeah!* And then you get your ass back here.'

'You got it, cowboy!' Franco grinned as he pocketed his gun and began filling a bag with the money. 'But what do you want me to come back for?'

'Because I need someone like you to protect me from…well…someone like you. I want to employ you as my bodyguard. And I'll pay you well.'

'How well?'

'A cool million a year, boy. Do we have a deal?'

Franco stopped stuffing the money away for a moment. He couldn't believe what he was hearing. That was more money than he could have ever imagined. He looked Earl in the eye and stuck out his hand. The two men shook on the deal.

'I'll see you in a few days, boss,' said Franco, 'and you won't be hearing from Don Romano again. I promise you that.' He gave Earl a wolfish grin as he disappeared into the darkness as lithely as a cat. He made his way downstairs and exited the ranch the same way he'd come in.

Earl sat on the edge of his bed and breathed a sigh of relief. That had been the scariest moment of his entire life.

*

Years on, the two men now had a close working relationship. Earl wasn't stupid enough to ever befriend or trust Franco, but he knew that so long as he was the highest payer, then Franco would be loyal to him. In return, Franco looked after his boss very carefully, accompanying him everywhere he went and taking care of any threats or problems that came his way.

As the senator finished his rally and came down off the stage, Franco went to his side and chaperoned him out of the exit door and into the back of the stretch limo parked just outside. The stretch limo could easily seat eight passengers in comfort. It was thirty feet long, dazzling white, and built with reinforced glass and steel to be completely bulletproof. It needed to be in Texas, where almost half the population carried a gun. Attached to the top of the vast front grille of the car was a pair of enormous buffalo horns. Under the hood was a mighty 5 litre V8 engine. Earl settled himself into the soft cream leather upholstery and helped himself to a glass of fine Kentucky bourbon from the onboard bar. Franco walked round to the driver's door, climbed in, and seated himself behind the steering wheel. Even though Franco was six feet seven inches tall, the limo was plenty big enough to accommodate his huge frame. He started the engine with a throaty roar, and the limo set off out of Galveston docks heading towards the i45 highway. The highway ran all the way back to Houston, where the offices of Lone Star Freight were located in the Downtown area of the city centre.

An hour later, the limo turned into the underground parking lot of the Lone Star Freight office block and pulled up into Earl's reserved space. The two men alighted from the car and made their way over to the elevator. They rode the elevator to the top floor, where Earl's private office suite was located. The top floor was forty storeys high and afforded fantastic panoramic views over Houston city centre. Earl and Franco walked briskly across the foyer and through the double wooden entrance doors of Earl's office. Inside, a smartly dressed woman was waiting for them, clipboard in hand. The lady's name was Lorna Wheeler, and she was Earl's private secretary. Earl went to sit behind his immense wooden desk while Franco stood to one side, resting his back against the floor to ceiling bookcases that were situated either side of the office. Earl hadn't read a single one of the books, but it sure looked impressive.

'I have your daily reports and bulletins ready, Senator,' came the businesslike voice of Lorna.

Earl removed his Stetson and placed it on the desktop carefully. He then smoothed out his toupee, which had become a little bit tangled up within the hat. Lorna tried not to stare and hid her smirk by biting her lip.

'Why, thank you, Lorna,' Earl boomed in his deep Texan drawl. 'What's the news today?'

'Stocks and shares are up three points,' replied Lorna. 'All freighters are running on schedule, and we've gained a new contract to ship oil from Venezuela to Mangalore in India.'

'*Can I do it?...Hell yeah!*' Earl bragged, looking mighty pleased with himself.

'It's not all good news, I'm afraid, Senator,' Lorna continued with a hint of trepidation.

'Whaddaya mean? What's the problem?'

'It's in regard to your takeover of the docks in Sunderland, England.'

'Oh, yeah?'

54

'They've called a strike,' Lorna informed him.

'*A strike!*' bawled Earl angrily. 'What in the name of Lincoln's beard have they called a goddamn strike for?'

'Some union man called Len Finch is concerned you're only out for profit and…'

'*Only out for profit!*' roared Earl. 'What kind of cockamamie businessman would I be if I wasn't out for profit?'

Lorna flicked through her notes.

'It says here he's concerned you're going to exploit his comrades,' she told him.

'*Comrades?*' exclaimed Earl in disbelief. 'Who is this guy? A goddamn commie?'

Lorna flicked through her notes again.

'Well, yes, practically…'

'What in the name of Godzilla's gizzards is going on over there?' he exclaimed in exasperation.

'No idea,' Lorna responded honestly, 'but we have had a communication from the Conservative Party candidate who is offering to help with the situation.'

Giles Wight had included a report in his notes to Alice about Earl's takeover of the docks. He'd also emailed her the news of the strike as soon as he'd heard. Alice had immediately consulted with her father about the matter. Between them, they'd decided it would be a great opportunity for the Tory party if they were to help with Lone Star's takeover of the docks. They'd sent a communique to the senator's offices in Houston forthwith.

'What in tarnation is the Conservative Party?' demanded Earl brusquely.

Jesus, doesn't this guy know anything? Lorna mused. 'They're like the equivalent of the Republicans in the United Kingdom,' she explained as simply as she could.

'Okay!' said Earl sounding hopeful. 'Now we're getting somewhere. Well, you get in touch with this guy and thank him for his assistance…'

'She's a woman.'

'*What?*'

'She's a woman. Her name is Alice Chesham.'

'I don't work well with women,' Earl stated flatly.

Franco allowed himself a knowing smile. He knew Earl wasn't lying. His relationships with women were legendarily disastrous and rarely lasted more than a few weeks. No woman could put up with his ultra-machismo approach to life for very long.

'Aw, come on now, boss,' Franco teased him, 'ain't you in touch with your feminine side?'

'I used to be,' replied Earl bluntly, 'but the bitch won't talk to me any more.'

Franco chuckled while Lorna rolled her eyes. She'd just about had enough of Earl too.

'What would you like me to do, Senator?' asked Lorna seriously.

Earl reached for his hat as he gave it some thought. He placed the Stetson firmly on his head as he rose to his feet.

'You tell Ms Chesham that I thank her for her assistance and I look forward to making her acquaintance. And you tell her that I'm a-coming to England in person to deal with this strike. And you tell her I'm gonna be *kicking some ass*!'

'Yes, sir,' affirmed Lorna. She hurried away to her own office to prepare the reply.

Earl turned his attention to his bodyguard.

'Franco, get the cars and the usual gear loaded on a next available freighter we have headed to England. You and me are going on a little sailing trip! Make sure everything is prepared. I want to be leaving first thing in the morning. Y'hear?'

'You got it, boss,' replied Franco. He sprang into action and went to make the necessary arrangements.

7.

Alice had driven up to Sunderland from Norfolk in her Mini Countryman and was staying in a hotel for the night in the city centre. She was due to meet Barry Higgins for lunch the following day so Barry could give her a bit of an induction before she formally took over the Conservative candidacy for the area. She had gone through Giles Wight's notes with a fine-tooth comb, trying to get a feel for her new constituency. She was very grateful to him for letting her know about the takeover in the docks and the upcoming trade union strike action. Following her father's advice, she'd contacted the office of Lone Star Freight and offered her assistance. It gave her a good opportunity to make an impression.

The following morning, after a light continental breakfast at the hotel buffet, she returned to her room to get ready. Checking her emails, she noted she'd had a reply from Lorna Wheeler, who was the secretary to the president of Lone Star Freight, Senator Earl Sanderson III. The email was a little forthright. She was pleased to see that they'd accepted her offer of assistance but she wasn't too sure what all the ass-kicking was all about. *How peculiarly American*, she mused. Anyway, apparently, he'd be arriving at Sunderland docks in one of his own freighters in about a week's time.

The restaurant where she was due to meet Barry had been recommended by Giles. It was a smart French bistro called Chez Marcel, located in one of the smaller avenues just off the city centre. She was due to meet him at 12:30pm. She had a few hours to spare so after checking out of the hotel, she decided to take a stroll around town. For one thing, she needed to pick up the keys for her rental flat from the letting agents. Carstairs had found the property for her and completed all the paperwork on her behalf. She was sure the flat would be lovely. Carstairs had impeccable taste.

She completed her mini tour of the city centre in good time. Picking up her flat keys en route, she then made her way to the restaurant. She arrived a little early, at 12:20, and was shown to her table by the charming waiter, Pierre. She was handed a menu, which she studied while she waited for Barry to arrive. The restaurant was bijou but chic, consisting of about a dozen tables, and was just starting to fill up with customers.

A few minutes past half twelve, the door to the restaurant opened gently, and a dishevelled looking Barry Higgins entered the bistro. Alice noted he looked totally different from when she'd last met him at the manor in Norfolk. Barry was wearing dark blue jeans with bright white trainers, and a tan-brown leather jacket covering a pale green polo shirt. His chubby midriff spilled out over the top of his jeans and his tousled hair looked as if it had been recently wetted and hastily combed into place. Recognising Alice instantly, he walked over to her table and shook her firmly by the hand before sitting down.

'How pet,' he said warmly, 'ees grand ter see yer agan. How ur ya deein?'

Alice was getting accustomed to the accent and slang. She'd been listening to some audio clips of Geordies talking and her ear was starting to get in tune. She could understand Barry a whole lot better now.

'I'm fine, Barry, thanks,' she replied. 'It's good to see you too.'

Just then, Pierre appeared at the table, armed with more menus.

'Bonjour, Monsieur,' he greeted Barry in a genteel French lilt. 'And 'ow are you today?'

'Oh, err, tres bien merci…er…bonjour,' said Barry, desperately trying to recall his rusty schoolboy French. He didn't want to appear uncouth in front of Alice.

Pierre smiled politely as he handed him the menus.

'Alors, le menú, Monsieur. Et la carte des vins. À bientôt.'

Pierre sashayed away again, leaving Barry looking perplexed.

Alice noticed Barry was staring at the menu in confusion.

'Is something wrong, Barry?' she asked with concern.

'Nar, nar,' said Barry, trying to be nonchalant. 'It's jus' the waiter's givun us the menu all in French, like. Ee must ha' thurt a wus from Paris or summat, y'knaa, after a wus chattin' wi' 'im in fluent French, like.'

Alice's eyes twinkled mischievously, and she had to purse her lips to stop herself from chuckling.

'Oh, I see,' she said, feigning sincerity. 'Well, I can help you with the translation if you like. I'm not too bad at French.'

'Oh nar. Nay wurries, lass. Me French's all cummin' back to me now, like. Piece o' cake.'

Pierre had rematerialised at the table again. This time with a pad and pen in hand ready to take the order.

'Madame is ready?' he enquired.

'Oui, merci. Une salade Niçoise, s'il vous plaît,' she answered neatly.

'Tres bien, Madame. And to drink?'

'Vin blanc. Chablis, if you have it.'

'But, of course, Madame.'

'Merci beaucoup.'

'Et pour Monsieur?' enquired Pierre, turning to Barry.

Barry was running his finger up and down the menu, rubbing his chin, and pretending he couldn't quite decide what to choose. In truth, there was only one thing on the menu he vaguely recognised. The rest of it might as well have been written in Mongolian.

'The steak, I think, por favor,' he finally decided.

Pierre winced slightly at the little Hispanic faux pas but politely carried on with the order.

'An excellent choice, Monsieur,' Pierre congratulated him. 'Le chef's *pièce de résistance.*'

Barry beamed proudly.

'And to drink, Monsieur? Red? White?...'

'Er, no. Brown, please.'

'Brown, Monsieur?'

'Aye, a brown ale, please.'

'Ah, mais oui. Of course, Monsieur.'

Pierre collected up the menus and hurried off into the kitchen to place the order with Marcel.

'This is a sweet little bistro, isn't it?' said Alice to start the conversation.

'Oh, aye. It's champion,' replied Barry. But then he looked around the room furtively and held his hand to his mouth in a secretive fashion. 'Mind you, I reckin' it's part o' a

61

chain, like. Seems to be owned by some fella called Gordon Bleu. I looked it up on t'internet. Ee mus' be loaded. His name's all over the place.'

'Gosh,' nodded Alice, going along with the story. 'Actually, I think I've heard of him.'

'There ye are, then,' said Barry, tapping his nose conspiratorially, having imparted this pearl of wisdom.

Pierre reappeared with the drinks and placed them down on the table.

'Santé,' he smiled at them before whizzing off again.

Alice took a sip of the crisp white Chablis and savoured the aroma with pleasure. Barry grasped his glass of ale and took a swig. Alice was surprised to see that almost half a pint had disappeared.

'Hoo, tha's hit the mark,' declared Barry with a small burp. 'Now, pet, would ye excuse us a moment, like. I wus oot on the toon last night wi' the boys fer a curry and sum ales, and av gorra bit o' Delhi belly, like. Mebbe had tay many ales 'n'all, if ya kna' worra mean!'

'Don't tell me you're a binge drinker, Barry?' Alice teased him.

'Nar. Don't be daft,' he replied, looking shocked. 'I drink loads *all the time*.'

He gave her a grin as he got to his feet. She grinned back. She'd never met anyone quite like Barry. Mind you, people said that about him all the time.

Barry stood up and then walked away from the table looking around for the cloakroom. He couldn't see where it was located. Luckily, Pierre was wandering past with a tray of drinks and saw Barry was looking puzzled.

'Tout va bien, Monsieur?' he asked.

Oh, no, thought Barry. *He still thinks I'm bloomin' French. Now what?* He racked his brains for the right French words, but they weren't coming readily into his brain.

'Er…j'aime…,' he tried.

Pierre raised an eyebrow.

'Er…er…j'aime…,' he tried again.

Pierre raised the other eyebrow.

Suddenly, the word he thought he was after pinged into his mind.

'Oh…er…j'aime…*merde*,' he said, pointing frantically at his bottom.

A look of distraught horror crossed Pierre's face.

But then understanding dawned into the Frenchman's mind.

'Les toilettes, Monsieur?'

'Oh, aye,' said Barry, relieved he'd been understood, 'Les twalets.'

'Behind the screen, Monsieur.' Pierre indicated the freestanding privacy screen located close to the far wall.

'Merci, Señor,' said Barry as he made his way over.

Behind the screen was a thin, wood veneered door marked with the familiar WC sign. Since the restaurant was so small, there was just the one shared cloakroom. It was no bigger than a broom cupboard, with a toilet on one side, and a wash hand basin on the other. But what more did you need? Barry hurried inside and closed the door behind him. Pulling his jeans down, he sat on the pan and made himself comfortable.

Back at the table, Alice had just taken another sip of her wine, when she thought she could detect the faint sound of someone singing. As she listened more intently, the singing appeared to be emanating from somewhere behind the privacy screen. And now the singing was getting quite a bit louder. She could even make out the lyrics, despite the broad accent.

'*Thou shalt have a fishy, on a little dishy,*' went the chirpy song…

'*Thou shalt have a fishy, when the boat comes in,*' it continued.

With growing panic, Alice realised that the voice belonged to Barry, and he was clearly oblivious to the fact that the entire restaurant could hear him through the paper-thin door. She prayed that the other customers would think the singing was coming from elsewhere. As she looked around the room, there were a few looks of bemusement on the faces of the other diners, but no one seemed that bothered. *Thank goodness*, she thought.

But, alas, Barry was only just getting into his stride and now began a lengthy running commentary as to exactly what was going on in his little world.

'Ooh, ya basta'd,' his voice rang out, slightly muffled, but still quite clearly from behind the screen. 'Tha' Vindaloo was red hot gan in and cummin' oot!'

There then ensued a noisy rattling sound as a ream of lavatory paper was unravelled from the roll.

'Reet,' came the voice again, 'let's get tha' lot off ter the coast!'

The sound of the toilet flushing was the next commotion to accost the senses, followed closely by water being run rapidly from a tap, and finally the scrunching of a paper towel as Barry dried his hands.

The faces of the guests were all singularly appalled. As they gazed at one another in astonishment and disgust, they all truly hoped that he was now finished, and the whole revolting episode was over.

'Aw, nar,' moaned the voice of Barry loudly from the WC, 'norra bloody floater!'

Presently, another torrent of lavatory paper could be heard being unfurled. His plan was to use the paper to sink the offending item. There was a short pause while Barry waited for the cistern to refill, then the toilet was flushed again.

'*Get down, Shep!*' was the command that could be heard being shouted sternly from behind the lavatory door. Shortly followed by a celebratory, '*Yes! Get in!*'.

Finally, after another brief pause, the toilet door was unlocked and Barry emerged from behind the screen and walked nonchalantly back across the restaurant. Barry noticed that, for some reason he couldn't fathom, everyone in the bistro seemed to be staring at him. He smiled graciously and nodded happily at them as he passed. Eventually he returned to the table where Alice was waiting and sat down again.

Alice had been busy examining the stitching on her napkin, which had suddenly become incredibly fascinating. As Barry sat down, she reluctantly put the napkin back on her knee.

'They're a funny lot in 'ere,' he said to her. 'What're they all sturrin' at me fer?'

'I really couldn't say,' Alice replied innocently.

'Well, noo,' he exclaimed, rubbing his hands together and changing the subject. 'How ur ye settlin' in? Did ye have a deek roond toon this marnin'?'

'Yes, I did. Only round the city centre, though. I didn't have time to go much further.'

'Aw, ees a canny toon is Sunderland. Ye'll soon get ta kna it.'

'I'm looking forward to learning all about it. I can't wait to make a start on the campaign either,' said Alice enthusiastically.

'Oh, aye. That reminds me. At the end o' next week, I've set up a little introduction fer ye to meet Alan Bailey, the lurcal MP. Alan's a reet class fella. A good pal o' mine, 'n'all. Anyhow, ee's invited yer ter mek a speech doon at the Dockers club. Along with 'im an' Len Finch, the union boss. All te dockers'll be there, 'n'all.'

'What's Len like?' queried Alice.

'Finch is a propa basta'd, ter be honest wi' ye. When I wos a docker, he were in charge. Always mekkin' trubble. Ye wanna watch oot fer 'im, lassee, ee's a sly one. And I can tell ye for nowt ee'll have it in for ye.'

'Thanks for the heads up, Barry.'

'Nay wurries.'

The conversation was interrupted by the arrival of the food. Pierre placed Alice's salad Niçoise down in front of her and then placed the steak in front of Barry.

Pierre pressed his fingertips to his lips and proclaimed, 'Bon appétit!'. He then disappeared back into the kitchen.

Alice picked up her knife and fork and was about to tuck in when she noticed that Barry was just sat looking forlornly at his plate.

'Is everything okay?' she enquired with concern.

'Well, it's a bit embarrassin', like,' said Barry.

'What is?'

'The steak.'

'Why?'

'Well, they've forgot ter cook the bugga,' explained Barry.

'They've forgotten to cook your steak tartare?' asked Alice, trying to keep a straight face.

'Aye. Friggin' unbelievable, innit?'

'Well, you'll have to send it back.'

'Oh, nar, I divvun't wanna cause a scene, like.'

Pierre was making his way back to the table to perform a check-back and saw with great concern that Barry had not touched his plate.

'Something is not to your liking, Monsieur?' he implored, wringing his hands anxiously.

'Erm, well it's a bit underdone fer my taste, like,' Barry clarified the situation. 'If ye could just stick it under ter grill fer a coupla minutes each side, that'd be grand.'

'Stick it under the grill, Monsieur?'

'Aye…and if ye could serve it up in a bap or summat, that'd be champion.'

'A *bap?!*'

'Could ye bung us some chips on, 'n' all?'

'Chips?'

'Oh, sorry, pal. I mean *French fries*.'

'French fries…,' whispered Pierre, a little piqued.

'Magic.'

'So, Monsieur, if I understand correctly, you wish to have your steak tartare served as a burger and chips? Oui?'

'Aw, nar, son. I wouldn't gae that far.'

Pierre tutted and trailed off miserably to the kitchen to put in the request.

'Burger an' chips! I ask ye! Common as muck, that one,' announced Barry, tilting his head towards the dejected waiter.

Suddenly, from the kitchen, there was a huge cacophony of smashing plates, and a terrific crash of pots and pans being hurled against the wall.

'*Qu'est-ce que c'est! Cochon Anglais!*' was bawled from the kitchen as the furious moustachioed face of Marcel appeared at the porthole window of the servery door. He peered through the glass with a crazed murderous look in his eye as he tried to spy the individual responsible for insulting his *haute cuisine*. Pierre was doing his best to calm him.

'Blimey,' said Barry with surprise. 'Someone's got outta bed the wrang side today!'

Alice was in a fit of giggles and could not control herself from laughing out loud. She just couldn't get it into her head how anyone could cause such complete and utter mayhem yet be so blithely unaware of it.

'Wha's tickled you, then?' asked Barry, looking puzzled.

'Oh, Barry,' she replied, wiping tears from her eyes. 'I think this is the beginning of a beautiful friendship.'

'I'll drink to that,' he said, beaming happily. He picked up his brown ale and clinked it with Alice's wine glass.

Pierre returned with Barry's order and plonked it down unceremoniously on the table.

'Smashin',' Barry proclaimed, eyeing his burger and fries with glee.

Pierre sighed sadly and turned to go back to the kitchen to console Marcel.

'Eh, pal, befer ye go,' said Barry, lightly grasping the waiter's arm. 'Would ye 'ave any ketchup?'

The waiter froze to the spot and hunched his shoulders in a fearful cringe. He stuck out a hand shaking with emotion.

'Please, Monsieur,' he beseeched. 'I can take *no more*.'

Pierre shuffled sadly across the restaurant and back through the swing door into the kitchen. Barry was sure he could hear crying.

Barry's baffled gaze had followed the Frenchman all the way back to the kitchen. Now he turned his eyes back to Alice and shrugged.

'Touchy bugga, wurn't he? he commented placidly.

Alice was set off in fits again.

*

The rest of the week passed by with nothing much else to note. Alice used the time to unpack and settle into her new flat. She also put in an appearance at the small, rented office that served as Tory HQ for the area. Barry was sat at his desk in the office, answering the phone, fielding letters, replying to emails and generally holding the fort.

One day, Barry had offered to take her around in his car to see more of the area. He drove, what he liked to call a

69

'vintage' Austin Montego that was somehow still running. According to Barry, it was highly collectable. They'd visited the hospital, the Stadium of Light, the Nissan car factory, and, of course, the docks.

Alice felt she was slowly beginning to get a feel for the place.

8.

The Lone Star freighter MS Yellow Rose was twenty miles offshore of the Sunderland docks when her captain radioed in to announce their imminent arrival. Sunderland Port Authority acknowledged the radio call and informed them that a pilot boat would be sent to the entrance of the docks to guide the freighter in. The Port Authority then advised Border Force of the impending arrival, who confirmed they would be sending a team down to the quayside.

The Port Authority were, of course, aware of the strike action currently in place under the instructions of the trade union. The union boss, Mr Finch, would allow a small team to work to unload some of the more personal effects from onboard MS Yellow Rose, but had refused point blank to unload any of the cargo. This information had just been relayed to Senator Earl Sanderson III, who was not best pleased.

The captain of the freighter rendezvoused with the pilot boat close to the fairwater marker buoy on the approach to the harbour entrance. He carefully followed the little pilot boat. He knew only too well how treacherous British waters could be. The underwater sand and mud banks moved regularly, and it would be foolhardy indeed to deviate from the pilot boat's course.

The pilot boat led them through the gap between the sweeping arms of the breakwaters, situated to the north and south of the harbour entrance. They then passed through the narrower old piers before bearing left into the cargo docks themselves. Eventually the huge freighter came alongside the quay wall where a mooring had been reserved near the gantry cranes. The securing lines, as thick as a man's arm, were thrown ashore and the dockers on land pulled the ropes tight and made them fast onto the huge cast iron mooring bollards concreted into the dockside.

The officials from Border Force, who'd been waiting in their Portakabin on the dockside, now came out and stood in a huddled group alongside the freighter. They addressed the captain of the freighter through a loudhailer. They'd gotten as far as 'Good morning' when to their surprise a hot-headed, foul-mouthed individual, all dressed up like Boss Hogg, appeared on the bridge and began to ferociously tear a strip off them.

'*You goddamn, no-good, lazy, limey sons of bitches!*' he bawled down at them. 'Now, you wait right there, y'hear, you dumbass mothers, because I'm coming down there with my associate, and you are going to get your asses kicked!'

Earl, unfortunately, had assumed the high-viz jacketed group were dock workers. The ones that were now in his employ. And was venting his frustration at their unwarranted strike action.

Now, as any seasoned traveller will tell you, shouting abuse at any country's Border Force officials is not a great idea. And these boys were no exception. Most of them were ex-Forces. They were tough, hardened men who were well used to dealing with all kinds of criminals. From drug runners to terrorists to people smugglers, and everything in between.

As Earl and Franco descended the gangway and stepped ashore, they were both taken aback when a rugged looking man with a steely-eyed glare broke away from the group and approached them. He was the officer in charge, and a former Royal Marine.

'You will both come with me,' he ordered directly.

'Now, just one darned minute, boy. Do you know who you're talking to?' hollered Earl, poking the officer in his chest with a finger. 'I'm Senator Earl Sanderson III, *of Texas*. I just bought this here facility and that makes me *your* boss. Geddit? Just who the hell do you think you are?'

'I am Chief Immigration Officer Bruce Delaney, sir. And frankly, I don't care if you're George bloody Washington himself. And you are definitely not my boss, sir. Because my boss is the head of state of the United Kingdom, His Majesty King Charles III.'

'Come again?' said Earl with some confusion. It was slowly beginning to occur to him that he may have just goofed.

'I repeat. You will both come with me,' instructed Officer Delaney. 'This way.'

A more subdued Earl and Franco followed the officer into the nearby Portakabin. Inside there were two more armed officers, a desk with a computer and scanner, a walkthrough metal detector machine, a mobile privacy screen, some plastic chairs, and a table with various items scattered on top.

'Passports, please,' requested Officer Delaney formally.

Earl and Franco reached into their respective jacket pockets and produced their passports. Bruce took them, passed them through the scanner and entered a few details on the computer.

'Thank you,' he said, handing them back their passports. 'And now if you could please step through the metal detector, we can commence with security checks.'

Earl and Franco exchanged worried glances and hesitated slightly.

'*Today*, please, gentlemen,' said Bruce gruffly.

Earl shrugged and walked confidently through the portal of the machine. A loud high pitch beep was emitted.

'Are you carrying any metal items on your person?' enquired Officer Delaney.

'Why, now I come to think of it, I sure am,' replied Earl cordially. 'The spurs on my boots, and the buckle on my belt. I'll take 'em off for you kind gents.'

Bruce noted the change in attitude of the American to being far more cooperative and pleasant.

'Please pass through the machine again,' instructed Bruce.

Earl did as he was told, but the same high pitch beep was emitted again.

'Okay. I'm going to have to pat you down,' Bruce told him. 'Please stand here and raise your arms.'

Earl walked over to Officer Delaney and slowly raised his arms. Bruce began the pat down under his arms and immediately found a suspicious bulge. He delved his hand into the inside of Earl's jacket and his fingers instantly wrapped around the butt of a large revolver. He pulled out Earl's Colt 45 and waved it in front of him.

'What's all this then?' asked Officer Delaney suspiciously.

'Oh, that,' said Earl dismissively. 'Just my little peashooter. I use it at my rallies oftentimes.'

Bruce depressed the cylinder release catch and inspected the contents. He withdrew one of the bullets and held it between his finger and thumb.

'This revolver is fully loaded with live ammunition,' he informed Earl.

'I sure hope so, boy. Ain't no use otherwise,' came the surprisingly frank reply.

'Okay, Wyatt Earp,' said Officer Delaney, 'take a seat for now.' Bruce indicated one of the plastic chairs. Earl sat down heavily and sighed with impatience.

'Is this gonna take long, boy?' he demanded. 'I'm a busy man.'

Bruce ignored him, placed the gun into one of the evidence containers laid out on the table, and turned his attention to the towering Franco. Bruce knew a dangerous man when he was staring one in the face, and Franco certainly set off all the warning bells.

'Your turn,' Bruce said to him, waving the big man towards the metal detector.

Franco was so tall that he had to duck slightly to fit under the top of the scanner. As he went through, the machine practically exploded with beeps, sirens and flashing lights.

'Well, what a surprise!' scowled Officer Delaney sarcastically. 'You got a peashooter too?'

Franco regarded him balefully. 'Maybe,' he uttered menacingly.

'Okay, I'll let you do the honours,' Bruce said, indicating another evidence container on the table.

Franco's enormous hand slipped into the inside of his black jacket and came back out very slowly holding his Beretta handgun. He placed it in the container.

'Right, sir…,' Bruce began but was quickly interrupted.

'I ain't done yet,' murmured Franco through gritted teeth.

The hand went into another pocket and produced a silencer. It too was placed in the container. Out of another pocket came a flick knife, from another, a brass knuckle duster, another, a throwing knife, then a wire garotte, and finally from a holster located in the small of his back came a single-shot Derringer.

Officer Delaney raised an eyebrow at the last item Franco produced.

'My insurance policy,' Franco explained.

'I see,' said Bruce. 'And what exactly were you planning to do with this little lot? Start World War III?'

'Wasn't plannin' nuthin',' came the terse reply. 'Just doin' my job. I'm the senator's security director and personal bodyguard.'

Chief Officer Delaney scratched his stubbly chin while he contemplated Franco's response. *It did explain, at least*, Bruce reasoned, *why he was armed to the teeth.*

'Take a seat, Al Capone,' he said to Franco, indicating another plastic chair next to Earl. Franco gave him a dark look but sat down next to his boss.

'Can we get outta here now, boy?' Earl tried his luck.

Bruce stared at the two men sat in front of him with barely concealed disbelief.

'Under the terms of The Terrorism Act 2006,' he apprised them, 'I am hereby placing you both under immediate arrest. I will be needing to report the matter to my superiors for further instructions. I will be making the call now from outside. You will wait here. Do not attempt to leave this building.'

It was transpiring to the senator that he might be in a spot of bother.

'Can I make a call to my representative in England?' enquired Earl, reaching for his mobile phone.

'You can,' replied Bruce, heading to the door. 'But make it quick.'

*

The Chief Officer had assumed the senator was calling a solicitor, but in fact Earl rang the number of the Conservative Party offices in Sunderland. Barry answered the call on the fourth ring.

'Ged murnin'.' His voice crackled badly due to the poor reception on Earl's phone. 'Oo canny 'elp ye?'

Great, thought Earl, *trust me to get connected to a non-English speaker.*

'Howdy,' he boomed down the phone. 'This is Senator Earl Sanderson speakin'. I need to talk urgently to a Ms Alice Chesham. *Do you understand?*'

'Pettin' yer three,' came the garbled response.

Earl desperately hoped he'd been understood. The line clicked several times and then a clipped, upper-class English lady's accent poured into his ear.

'Alice Chesham speaking. How may I be of assistance?'

'Thank the Lord!' Earl exclaimed in relief. 'Ma'am, allow me to introduce myself. My name is Senator Earl Sanderson III, and your office was in touch with my secretary at Lone Star Freight in Texas about a week ago. I'm sure happy to make your acquaintance.'

'Thank you very much,' said Alice, somewhat taken aback with his forthright manner. 'Have you arrived safely at the docks, Senator? I do hope you had a fair crossing.'

'I have just this moment safely arrived, ma'am, but my colleague and I find ourselves currently detained on the dockside by your Border Force officials.'

'Oh, dear,' sympathised Alice. 'Is there a problem with the paperwork?'

'You might say that, yes,' continued Earl, telling a little white lie. 'And I'd be much obliged of your assistance if you could spare the time.'

'Oh right. Would you like me to come down to the docks and see what I can do?' she asked helpfully.

'I sure would appreciate it!' said Earl gratefully.

'I'll be down in about twenty minutes,' said Alice and hung up. She reached for her coat and handbag and set off out of the office.

'Weer ur ye gan?' quizzed Barry.

'To the docks,' explained Alice, 'to help our American friends. See you later.'

'Reet ye ur, lassee. Laters then.'

*

Chief Immigration Officer Delaney re-entered the Portakabin, having reported the situation to the Regional Director. He had his fresh orders. The Director had been extremely concerned by the infraction, given that firearms had been involved.

78

'Who had the highest authority with regard to your actions upon arrival in the United Kingdom?' demanded Officer Delaney.

'Come again?' said Earl, a little confused.

'Who's in charge? Who's the boss? The head honcho?'

'Why, I am, of course!' said the senator, rising to his feet with indignation.

'Well, congratulations!' proclaimed Bruce with a slight sneer. 'You win star prize.'

'What prize, boy?'

'A full cavity search!'

The senator thought he understood the Officer's meaning and nodded convivially.

'Okay. You mean you want to search the hold of my freighter?'

'Not exactly,' grimaced Officer Delaney, snapping a rubber prophylactic glove onto his right hand.

The action had not gone unobserved by Earl, who had just broken into a cold sweat.

'Now what in the name of Ezekiel do you think you're gonna do with that glove, boy?'

'My orders are to search you for hidden drugs. It's best not to struggle,' Bruce advised him, reaching for the lubricating gel.

The senator had backed up against the wall close to where Franco was sitting. 'Help me, for crying out loud,' he pleaded to his bodyguard.

The machine guns of the other two Border Force officers were immediately lowered and pointed at Franco.

'No can do, boss,' said Franco shrugging helplessly, although he was quite enjoying watching the senator squirm.

Officer Delaney bore down on Earl. 'Let's get this over with, sir,' he ordered sternly. 'Move over behind the privacy screen and drop 'em!'

Reluctantly Earl made his way across the room and behind the screen. He unfastened his belt, lowered his trousers and bent over slightly. As the gloved Bruce approached, he tried to appeal to Officer Delaney's better nature one last time.

'Now, if I was gonna smuggle drugs boy, I'd hide them on board my freighter, right? Why in the name of General George Custer would I shove 'em up my A-hooooooole.......'

But the deed was done as he spoke. And his protests were in vain.

*

Ten minutes later, Alice pulled her Mini Countryman into the Sunderland docks car park. She got out of the car and walked the short distance to the quayside. She could see the huge US flagged freighter moored up by the cranes, and, beside it, the Portakabin used by Border Force for processing new arrivals. She assumed this is where she would find Senator Sanderson.

She knocked lightly on the metal door and waited. It was opened within a few seconds and she was shown inside by the immigration officer in charge. He gave his name as Bruce Delaney. She noted two men sat against the far wall. One was dressed in a western style suit with a cowboy hat, while the other was all in black. Both men were large, but the man in black was simply enormous. And the way he was staring at her scared her a little. As Alice acknowledged them, the man with the cowboy hat stood up and started to walk towards her. She noticed he had a particularly strange walk. He waddled towards her like a bow-legged duck.

'Hey boss,' smirked the man in black. 'You're walking just like a saddle-sore cowboy!'

The man in the cowboy hat stopped in his tracks, and with a face set in fury, he turned his head back to reply to his colleague.

'So would you be, if you'd had folk rooting around in your cornhole!' He turned back to Alice. 'My apologies, ma'am. I'm Senator Earl Sanderson, by the way. We spoke on the phone. I thank you for coming over so quickly.'

Alice proffered a hand, which the senator took and shook firmly. She then turned to look at Officer Delaney.

'What's been going on here? Why are these men detained?' she asked directly.

'They attempted to bring firearms and other weaponry into the country,' explained Officer Delaney.

'And just what the hell is the problem with that?' implored Earl.

'Well, it happens to be illegal,' Alice told him.

'*Illegal?*' Earl was baffled. 'Ain't it every man's God given right to bear arms?'

'In Texas, maybe,' she replied. 'But definitely not in England.'

'Well, King Kong's Dong, if I ain't heard it all now!' he declared loudly. 'But listen up one darned minute…my associate over yonder is also my personal bodyguard. So,

81

answer me this: If someone's bothering me here in England, how in the name of PT Barnum is he supposed to blow them away?'

Officer Delaney and Alice caught each other's eye momentarily. Both were astonished.

'Well, he's not allowed to,' said Alice simply.

The senator was struggling to grasp the concept. *So, you can't shoot people in England*, he mused to himself. *This was all too weird.*

'Okay,' he tried again. 'So, let's say, *in England*, one of you guys has a problem with someone who's bad. Someone real nasty who's been wronging you. You get me? How do *you* deal with it, huh?'

Alice gave the problem some serious thought before replying.

'Well,' she said solemnly. 'You could try writing them a jolly stiff letter.'

A pause hung in the air momentarily as this information was processed.

'*A jolly stiff letter*,' the senator repeated slowly.

'And if you really mean it, you could get your solicitor to sign it too,' added Alice.

'Wow,' said Earl incredulously. 'Franco?'

'Yes, boss?' replied the bodyguard, sitting up in his chair.

'Have you ever tried writing a jolly stiff letter to say…the Triads…or the Mafia?'

'I don't think so, boss.'

'And did you ever involve a solicitor in any way?'

'No, boss.'

'Well, that's probably where we've been going wrong,' said the Senator sardonically.

'Okay, okay,' interrupted Officer Delaney, who could see where this was headed. 'What I think the lady is trying to point out is that if you have a problem of that nature in the United Kingdom, you don't just go around blowing people away. You would call the police and they will deal with the situation.'

'I hear your police don't have guns,' stated Franco.

'Of course they have guns!' retorted Officer Delaney. 'They just don't carry them with them. That's all'

'Well, that's very sporting of them,' noted Franco. 'Why do they do that? Do they like to give the crooks a fighting chance or something?'

Chief Officer Delaney actually found himself stumped for a reply to this one.

'Erm, well it's just not very nice to see, is it?' he said lamely.

'*Not very nice?*' commented the senator. 'What kind of cockamamie country is this?'

'One with very low gun crime,' pointed out Alice succinctly.

Now the senator and Franco were stumped for a reply.

'Anyways,' said Earl, changing tack. 'Can you help us get out of here, ma'am?'

Alice looked enquiringly at Officer Delaney.

'My orders are to detain them until further notice,' he told her.

Alice pondered the problem momentarily and then an idea came into her mind.

'Let me make a call,' she said confidently to Earl and Franco. 'I'm sure this can be resolved amicably and quickly.'

She stepped back outside of the Portakabin, fished out her mobile phone and began dialling her father's number. She didn't want the others to overhear the conversation. Eventually Humphrey answered the phone.

'Alice, darling,' he greeted her. 'How's things going up north?'

'Hello, Pater,' she replied. 'Got a bit of a favour to ask, to be honest.'

'Oh,' said Humphrey, sounding concerned. 'Is everything all right?'

'It's concerning Senator Sanderson,' she informed him, and filled him in on all the details. He listened carefully before replying.

'Well, there's nothing I can do about it, Alice, I'm afraid. I don't have any clout in that department.'

'I know, Pater, but you do know the Chancellor of the Duchy of Lancaster quite well now, don't you?'

'Oh yes, we get along famously.'

'Right. And surely, he knows the Home Secretary?'

'Well, yes…ah, I get your drift,' he said as the penny dropped. 'I'll call him right now. Clever girl.'

'Thanks, Pater. I owe you big time,' she said and hung up with a smile.

While Alice waited for her father to call back, she took the opportunity to look around the docks. She noted the harbour entrance, the gantry cranes and containers, and across the other side of the water she could just see the working men's club where she was due to give a speech in a few days' time. She also noticed that there was no work going on, courtesy of Mr Finch. It was a crying shame.

Her phone began ringing and she answered straight away. It was her father calling back.

'Good news,' he enthused. 'The Chancellor has spoken to the Home Secretary, and he's well aware of the importance of Senator Sanderson. He's sending an email communiqué to Sunderland Border Force as we speak. Ask the officer in charge to check his computer in a few minutes.'

'Thanks, Pater, you're the best,' she said appreciatively.

'Any time. Now I must dash. Let me know how you get on.'

'Will do.'

Once they'd hung up, she waited a few minutes further to give time for the communiqué to come through. After five minutes had elapsed, she re-entered the Portakabin. Senator Sanderson looked up hopefully from where he was seated. Alice gave him a confident nod.

'Officer Delaney,' she said sweetly 'would you mind checking your computer for any messages?'

'Really?' he asked sceptically.

'Really.'

He rolled his eyes but did as he was requested. He walked over to the security computer near the entrance door and logged in. He then checked for messages. To his surprise there was one in his inbox. And it wasn't any old message. It was a fully encrypted communiqué which bore the official seal of the Home Secretary. He began the program which decrypted high security missives and opened the communiqué.

85

To his growing consternation the contents of the message were strict instructions to treat the two Americans as though they were visiting VIP dignitaries. They were to be afforded every possible courtesy and not to be hindered or inconvenienced in any way. As Bruce Delaney spied the box of rubber gloves and jar of lubricant still sat on the table, his throat went rather dry and a bead of sweat appeared on his forehead. He continued to read the message. It did, at least, instruct him to confiscate any weapons. Thank God he'd got that right. He rapidly closed down the messaging program and turned off the computer. He stood up straight and pulled himself together. Everyone was looking at him expectantly.

'Ahem,' he began with just a hint of nervousness. 'I have hereby received instructions to release Senator Earl Sanderson III and Mr Franco Gambini with immediate effect.'

'About time, boy,' snapped the senator irritably. 'Now, can I have my Colt 45 back?'

'I regret to inform you, sir' said Bruce stiffly,' that all weaponry will remain confiscated until you clear customs on your departure. It will then be returned to you on board your vessel.'

'Aw, hot damn!' railed the senator. 'Well, now what am I supposed to do? My Colt is like a part of me. I ain't the same man without my gun. I gotta have me one!'

While Chief Officer Delaney turned away to sign off some paperwork, Alice touched the senator's shoulder lightly to get his attention.

'I might be able to find you a replica gun, Senator,' Alice whispered discreetly to him. 'But it will certainly not fire real bullets.'

'Aw, gee whizz!' complained Earl, like a spoilt child. He pulled a sullen face. 'Well, if that's all I can get...I suppose so.'

'I'll see what I can do,' she informed him. 'And now, shall we get out of here?'

The senator brightened at that idea.

'Darn tootin'!', he whooped. 'And I'm much obliged for your assistance, Ms Chesham. You're a very capable woman, I can see that.'

'You're very welcome, Senator,' she beamed.

They walked together out of the Portakabin and onto the dockside. While they'd been detained, the dockers had unloaded three containers off the freighter and placed them carefully on the quayside. The gantry cranes had lifted the metal containers using a giant magnet as a hoist. The captain of the freighter had been supervising the process. Each container held one of Earl's precious stretch limos inside. The senator always travelled with at least three of these vehicles in his cavalcade. On their private registration plates, they were aptly named Earl I, Earl II and Earl III. The trade union had given permission to use the gantry cranes to offload the cars, but that was all. No cargo was permitted to be offloaded. With the work complete, the dockers made off across the other side of the water and disappeared into the working men's club.

'Where will you be staying on your visit?' Alice asked Earl.

'Right here,' answered Earl, indicating the freighter. 'I have a very comfortable suite of rooms on board.'

'I see,' said Alice. 'Very sensible. And I see you've brought your own transport.'

'Hell, yeah!' drawled Earl proudly. 'Wouldn't go nowhere without my limos. I like to travel in style! We'll probably take a drive out tomorrow. Perhaps you'd care to join us and we can discuss business further?'

'By all means,' agreed Alice, happy to have gained the senator's trust. 'Well, I'll leave you now to get settled in, and I'll come by again in the morning. What time would you like me here?'

'Shall we say ten o'clock?'

'Perfect,' said Alice politely. 'See you then.'

Earl grinned and tipped his Stetson in friendly acknowledgement. Even Franco managed to crack a smile.

*

On her way back to the office Alice dropped by a toy shop she'd seen while exploring the city centre a few days ago. She enquired of the assistant is he had any realistic looking cowboy style handguns. The shop had actually had a pretty impressive collection of toy guns and it'd been hard to decide which was best. In the end, she'd purchased the "Sheriff's Revolver" which looked the most similar to Earl's Colt 45. It was made of shiny metal with a sturdy wooden handle, had a revolving cylinder that could be ejected to the side, and was capable of firing the largest caps available in the UK market. She'd bought half a dozen packets of the caps to go with it. The assistant had given her a demonstration and Alice had been quite shocked how loud the caps were. In fact, the only thing that really distinguished it from a real gun was the red plastic bung fixed into the barrel to indicate, in no uncertain terms, that it was a toy replica.

When she returned to the office, she'd told Barry all about what had happened and how she'd managed to get the senator out of trouble. Barry had been made up for her. She also told him that she'd been invited the following day to accompany the Americans on a drive around in one of Earl's stretch limos.

'Howay, man,' said Barry avidly. 'I'm deed jealous o' ye. I've urlways wanted to gan in one o' them, like.'

'I'll put in a good word for you, Barry,' Alice promised.

'How, pet, but yer a class lass,' he said happily.

9.

The next morning, Alice pulled up at the docks and walked the short distance along the quayside to where the US freighter MS Yellow Rose was moored up. One of the stretch limos, the one named Earl I, had been driven out of its container and was parked up next to the gangway, ready to be driven off. The huge vehicle was gleaming white and Alice was especially impressed with the blacked-out windows, the vast sunroof, and the colossal buffalo horns attached to the front grille. She'd never seen anything quite like it.

'Ain't she a beauty?' came a booming Texan drawl from the top of the gangway. It was the senator. 'Wait until you see inside!'

He marched down the gangway and joined Alice in admiring the fabulous limousine. Alice noticed he was walking a lot straighter this morning. He pulled a key fob from his pocket and clicked the button to unlock the car doors. He flipped the door handle on one of the doors, located roughly in the centre of the limo, and opened the door wide so Alice could see the interior. As Alice peered inside, she could see a large L-shaped sumptuous, cream leather sofa fitted on one side, all lit up with tiny lights fixed in the roof. Set in the opposite side was a minibar, a small desk and a state-of-the-art entertainment unit. In the centre of the roof was the huge glass sliding sunroof.

'Wow, that's awesome!' exalted Alice, trying to impress Earl by sounding American.

'Well, don't just stand there, girl. Slide on in and make yourself comfortable,' directed Earl courteously. 'Franco's just on his way, and then we'll get going.'

Alice climbed in, slid to the far end, and settled herself on the luxurious leather seat. Earl followed suit and sat in the centre of the sofa so he could easily reach the entertainment console. He began fiddling with the buttons and presently some country and western music started playing softly from the hi-fi system.

While they waited, Alice extracted the cap gun from her handbag. She'd removed it from the children's packaging so as not to embarrass the senator. The box it had come in had been clearly labelled for ages 3+, which would have been a bit awkward. Instead, she'd wrapped it in some padded packaging paper that she'd had left over from moving into her flat.

'I bought a replica handgun for you yesterday afternoon,' said Alice handing him the package. 'I hope it will suffice.'

'Why, thank you, ma'am,' replied Earl, eagerly accepting the gift. 'That's mighty kind of you.'

The senator was as giddy as a child on Christmas Day as he unwrapped the package. His eyes lit up as he saw the handgun and he picked it up in his hand to feel the weight. He wasn't disappointed. It was a little light, but it sure looked fine.

Alice showed him how to break the barrel and load the cylinder with the caps.

'Now, obviously they're only blanks,' she explained,' but they're pretty loud, I can tell you!'

Just then, Franco appeared at the top of the gangway and began to walk down it to the quayside. Alice was staggered that such a big man could move so agilely.

Earl opened the electric window of the limo and, with a childlike snicker, took aim at Franco with the gun. He fired several shots at him in quick succession. The senator was heartily satisfied with the convincing gunshot sound made by the replica. Franco's trained killer instincts immediately cut in, and thinking himself the target of an assassination attempt, he nimbly leapt behind some nearby oil drums and took cover.

Earl fell about, laughing hysterically. He stuck his head out of the car window and bawled at his bodyguard.

'Hey, Franco – I gotcha'!'

Franco's head materialised from round the side of the oil drums.

'Whatcha' shooting at me for, boss? I done something wrong?'

'Nah! Come on out, boy!' hollered Earl. 'They're just blanks!'

Franco stood up and dusted himself down. He walked over to the limo and bent down to peer through the window.

'Let me see that thing,' he murmured inquisitively.

'Not bad, huh?' said Earl handing him the gun. 'Ms Chesham here acquired it for me.'

Franco was turning the gun round in his hands. He noted the red bung stuck in the barrel.

'What's that for?' he asked.

'So folk know it only fires blanks, I guess,' responded Earl.

Franco held the red bung between his thumb and finger and gave it a twist. It snapped off as easily as breaking a dry twig.

'Not any more,' he grunted, handing the gun back to his boss.

Alice was looking on with concern. She wasn't sure that was such a good idea.

Earl put the gun away in the holster under his arm and pocketed the packages of caps.

'Okay, Franco, get yourself in the driver's seat and let's get rolling,' he ordered.

'You got it, boss,' Franco replied and lumbered off to settle himself behind the wheel.

Presently they felt the engine rumble to life and the limo slowly set off along the dockside, heading for the main road.

'Where do you recommend we go?' Earl asked Alice.

'Well, what would you like to see?' Alice responded. 'City lights or the countryside?'

'I'm a country boy at heart,' said Earl. 'And I'd sure love to see some of the famous English countryside. I hear it's real quaint.'

'Absolutely,' chimed Alice. 'Why don't we head out towards the Pennines? I think you'll find it stunningly picturesque.'

Earl pressed a button on the desk, which was actually an intercom connected to the driver's cabin.

'Franco,' he shouted into the intercom.

'I hear you, boss.'

'Set the sat-nav for *the Pennines*! We're going into the country!'

'Yes, sir!' came Franco's voice back through the intercom.

As the car wound its way onto the main road and headed out of the city towards the countryside, Alice and Earl settled back in their seats to enjoy the ride. They began to make polite conversation but it wasn't long before the conversation turned to business, and in particular, the problem of the strike action in the docks. Alice quickly deduced it was something that was intensely bothering the senator, and his anger in the matter was barely concealed. Earl wanted to deal with the matter with all guns blazing (as it were), but Alice was trying to push for a more measured approach. She felt the way to beat Mr Finch was to play him at his own game and make it impossible for the strike action to continue. She had ideas of implementing environmentally friendly technology to the business which would force the union to back down. Earl, on the other hand, wanted to shout down the trade union boss, threaten the dockers with being fired, and, as he liked to put it, *kick some ass*.

After much debate they agreed that Earl would try his way first, and Alice's plan would be the back-up. In the circumstances, she didn't have much choice but to agree. At least he'd taken her comments on board. At any rate, they were making some progress to resolving the situation.

As Alice and Earl paused the conversation for a moment, they both looked out of the window to admire the scenery. The limo had left the motorway and they were now travelling down a smaller A-road. As they left the built-up areas behind them, the view was rapidly becoming more scenic.

Franco was enjoying the drive too. It was the first time he'd driven on the left side of the road, and it felt very strange. However, he was soon getting accustomed to it. The sat-nav, set for *the Pennines*, whatever they were, had directed him off the motorway and onto a much smaller road, which he could see was referred to as an A-road in England. After several miles the sat-nav was telling him to make a further turn onto something called a B-road. Franco followed the instructions and found himself on a road that he would describe as a single-track lane. Given the size of the limo, to all intents and purposes, it might as well have been a one-way street. And this was exactly how Franco intended to treat it. He got away without any approaching traffic for a couple of miles, but now a vehicle hove into view several hundred yards ahead. As it came closer, he could see it was an old green Land Rover being driven by an aged fellow wearing a flat cap. Unsure of the correct procedure in a situation such as this, Franco thought his best bet was to resort to giving the approaching vehicle a good blast of the car horn. Now, this being Earl's limo, the car horn wasn't any old car horn. *Hell, no!* The senator's mechanic had modified the car horn to play the first two bars of *The Star-Spangled Banner*. At 120 decibels. About the same volume as an ambulance siren.

As Franco sounded the horn, the unfortunate driver of the Land Rover nearly soiled himself in terrified surprise and then veered erratically off the road and onto the verge. As the limo swept past, the poor old fellow was left gasping for breath and shaking with shock.

'Hey!' shouted Alice with concern. 'I think we just ran someone off the road!'

Earl hurriedly pressed the intercom button.

'Franco! What the hell are you doing, boy?' he demanded.

A stressed voice came back over the intercom. 'I didn't know what else to do, boss. This road's so goddamn narrow – I had to do something! Aw gee, there's another one coming.'

The car horn blared again and this time an estate car with a family of four was barged off the road and into a nearby field.

95

Alice grabbed the intercom off Earl. 'Franco, for heaven's sake, you don't have to keep sounding the horn like that! Drivers in Britain will pull over and let you pass. You'll see…'

'They will?' came the surprised reply.

'Yes! Just slow down a bit and give them a chance to pull over, that's all you have to do!' cried Alice in frustration.

'Oh, okay. I'll try that.'

Sure enough, when the next car approached, Franco slowed down, and the oncoming car found a spot to pull over and keep out of the way. As Franco drove the limo past, the driver of the car even gave him a friendly little wave.'

'What's she waving at me for?' asked Franco, a little perplexed.

'She's just being polite,' explained Alice. 'You're supposed to wave back.'

'You want me to wave at people?'

'It's just what we do in Britain.'

'Well, it freaks me out,' complained Franco.

'Just do it, Franco!' ordered Earl.

'Okay, okay!' came the tetchy reply.

As they continued their progress down various country lanes, oncoming cars courteously pulled over, the limo swept statelily by, and cute little waves were pleasantly exchanged. Although Franco would never admit it, after six or seven times, he was actually starting to enjoy the little tradition. It was all so civilised and quaint.

They were now starting to climb up into the hills of the Pennines. They passed through achingly pretty stone villages, complete with beautifully presented village greens and ponds. In one such village they stopped for lunch in a traditional country pub. They'd had a little trouble fitting the limo into the car park, but the pub wasn't busy, and they eventually managed to park up, drawing a small crowd of curious onlookers in the process.

Earl and Franco were amazed at the traditional interior of the pub, with its low beamed ceilings and huge open fireplaces. When Earl had walked up to the bar to place their food order, he took a good look at what drinks were available and was immediately fascinated with all the different types of beer that were on offer. There were lagers, bitters, and stouts on draught, and many other kinds of bottled beer, including brown ale, pale ale and IPAs. But he was especially intrigued by the old-fashioned real ales that were hand pumped up from casks in the cellar. He even tried a pint of one called Poacher's Potion. To his surprise the beer was light brown in colour. And it wasn't clear, it wasn't cold and it wasn't fizzy. When he took a sip, he found the taste to be bitter, hoppy, and almost nutty. It was also very strong in alcohol. Nothing like the beer he was used to. He didn't find it unpleasant, but it would sure take some getting used to, if he were being totally honest.

'That's one crazy strong brew you got there,' he commented cheerfully to the barman.

'It certainly is, mate,' smiled the landlord.

While he waited for the food, he chatted amiably to the barman, who was only too happy to while away the time talking to Earl. They didn't get many American tourists in this neck of the woods.

'How's your beer going down?' enquired the barman.

Earl took another gulp of the Poacher's Potion.

'The boys back in Houston will never believe me when I tell them about this *real ale*,' he smiled.

'I'll bet!' the landlord chuckled. There was the pinging of a bell from the kitchen. 'Your lunch orders are ready, pal. I'll bring them over.'

Earl rejoined Alice and Franco at their table by the window.

They'd all ordered fish and chips, which the landlord was now bringing over to their table.

'Enjoy,' he said as he placed the food down.

The fish and chips were excellent. The Americans were enjoying their day out and Alice was pleased they were all getting along. All too soon, it was time to head back.

Exiting the pub, they piled back into the limo and Franco pulled the huge car out of the car park and back on the road. He'd set the sat-nav to take them back to Sunderland docks. As often with sat-nav systems, the route back was different from the one they'd used to arrive. But armed with his newfound slowing down and waving technique, Franco was confident of dealing with anything the English country roads could throw at him. To their pleasant surprise the route back was even more scenic than before. They were passing over lots of little streams, brooks, and burns. The traditional bridges crossing over them were all constructed of stone, and most were centuries old.

As they meandered their merry way back, Franco saw a road sign he'd not encountered before. Seems like they were going to pass over yet another stream, only the upcoming bridge was something called a *humpback bridge* and appeared to warrant a warning sign. He couldn't for the life of him think why, so he just pressed on, confident in the knowledge that he could probably just wave his way out of trouble.

As he approached the bridge, he noted it was very narrow and only one vehicle could pass at a time. There was a car coming the other way, so he slowed down a little and, as expected, the car pulled over and stopped to allow him to cross the bridge. He crept the limo over the bridge, observing, belatedly, how steep it was on each side. *Now* he realised what *humpback* meant!

The front wheels of the limo cleared the ridge and then hung in the air, spinning madly. Then, a loud squealing sound of tortured metal could be heard as the undercarriage of the car was scraped along the tarmac on top of the bridge. The momentum of the vehicle carried it about halfway along its length, where it promptly came to a crunching, shuddering and abrupt halt. The rear wheels were also now free of the ground and spinning freely. The centre of the limo, subsequently, became a fulcrum, and the car rocked gently back and forth, like a seesaw, on the apex of the bridge. In a blind panic, Franco tried flooring the accelerator, but it was to no avail. There were no wheels in contact with the road. The limo was well and truly stuck.

'Shit,' said Franco, and thumped the car horn in frustration. The *Star-Spangled Banner* anthem was duly belted out at top volume, startling the elderly lady driver who had kindly pulled her car over.

Realising her predicament and seeing there was no way through, the lady huffily started her car and began to execute an angry three-point turn. As she did so, Franco saw her apparently waving at him. It was a strange wave though, as she was holding only her index finger and middle finger up in a kind of V shape and flicking them at him. Franco assumed it was something to do with Victory in the war, and she was wishing to convey her heartfelt thanks to the Americans for their wartime help. He imitated her V sign and coyly waved his fingers back at her, feeling a little foolish. She then mouthed a name at him. Franco was no expert at lip reading but she seemed to have him mistaken for someone called Stuart Tucker. She then sped off back the way she came.

Franco sighed and opened the driver's door slowly. There was a drop of a couple of feet to the road, so he hopped down, being careful not to injure himself. He went to the centre of the car and opened the door where Earl and Alice were sitting. He was immediately confronted with Earl's furious face.

'What in the name of Davy Crockett's furry hat do you think you're doing, boy?'

'Sorry, boss. I didn't know what a humpback bridge was…', replied Franco feebly.

'Well, now what are we going to do?' Earl fumed.

'I'll have to call the authorities,' said Alice, making the decision for them. 'It's all we can do.'

While they waited for the police and emergency recovery services to arrive, they sat on the stone bridge wall and looked dejectedly at the stricken limo. As the road was effectively blocked in both directions, a hefty line of cars was beginning to build up on both sides of the bridge. The line grew longer and longer and before long was beginning to affect larger roads in the area. Within an hour or so, a large section of the Pennines was gridlocked.

Half an hour later, a police motorcyclist followed by a recovery low-loader finally managed to fight their way through the lines of traffic and reach the scene.

The policeman dismounted from his motorcycle, removed his crash helmet and tried to take in the picture. He'd never had to deal with a problem like this before. He turned to the recovery mechanic for help.

'Any ideas?' the policeman asked him.

The mechanic scratched his head woefully. He was used to recovering cars, not stretch limos.

'It's too big to fit on the low-loader, that's for sure,' he replied.

'What are we going to do, then?'

'The only thing we can do…chop it up!' the mechanic said, starting to walk back to his truck.

He returned a minute later bearing an industrial-grade 9" angle grinder.

The senator was watching the duo with concern. When the mechanic started the angle grinder and marched purposefully towards his cherished limo, he felt he had to intervene. He stood up and barred the way.

'Now where do you think you're going with that buzzsaw, boy?' he challenged the mechanic.

'Out of the way, JW Pepper!' responded the mechanic in annoyance. 'You've caused enough aggro for one day.'

The policeman placed a hand on Earl's shoulder to restrain him.

'Your insurance company will cover it, sir,' he tried to console Earl. 'There's nothing else for it, I'm afraid.'

With a shrug, Earl backed down and watched forlornly as the mechanic reached the centre of the limo. Starting at the roof, he wielded the angle grinder expertly, cutting through the metal like a hot knife through butter. A large throng of bystanders, who had left their cars, were gathered watching the brutal operation with morbid glee.

The sides of the car look a little longer to cut through. Once this was done, the vehicle split open a little so the crowd could see the luxurious interior. They oohed and aahed in admiration.

Earl requested that the mechanic halt proceedings for a minute. Once the angle grinder had been switched off, Earl reached an arm into the limo and opened the drinks cabinet.

He fumbled around inside and came out holding a bottle of finest Kentucky bourbon.

'Might as well drown my sorrows with the good stuff,' he murmured sadly. Clutching the bottle, he went back to sit on the stone wall, taking a good swig of the bourbon as he did so. He passed the bottle to Franco who likewise took a slug out of the bottle. The bourbon was then offered to Alice, but she shook her head and declined.

'I'm going to call my associate, Barry, to come and pick us up. Otherwise, we're going to be stuck here.'

'Much obliged, *again*, ma'am,' Earl uttered, saluting her with the bottle.

While the two Americans drank away their woes, Alice rang Barry and asked him to make his way over to them as fast as he could. She warned him the roads would be very busy. Barry had said he'd set off right away.

The mechanic re-started the angle grinder and began cutting through the floor of the car. The metal here was a lot thicker and was taking him a good deal longer, but after twenty minutes of hard work, the job was done. The stately limo was split in two.

Using the low-loader's hoist, the mechanic was now able to lift the two pieces onto the recovery truck, one on top of the other. He secured the wreckage with some hefty straps and chains. Satisfied all was safe and secure, he climbed into the cab, started the engine and waited for the policeman to escort him back through the traffic.

The policeman handed Earl his incident report for insurance purposes. Earl took the piece of paper, folded it and put it in his jacket.

'Do you need any further assistance?' the policeman enquired. 'I can arrange a taxi for you, if you like.'

'Thanks,' said Alice, 'but I've called a friend to come and pick us up. I'm sure we'll be fine.'

The policeman nodded and then headed back to his motorcycle. He started the engine and turned on the blue flashing lights. He pulled up in front of the recovery truck, gave the mechanic a thumbs up, and they then both set off back through the traffic.

Now the bridge was unblocked, cars began to take it in turns to pass over the bridge, and the traffic began to move again. It took an hour and a half for the road to clear and return to any kind of normality. Forty-five minutes after that, Alice spied Barry's Austin Montego, smoke sporadically pouring out of the back, approaching their location. As he pulled up next to them the car backfired with a loud bang and then came to a halt. Barry wound down the driver's side window with a concerned look on his face.

'Are ye url areet?' he asked apprehensively. 'Wurs the limo gan, then?'

'Don't ask,' replied Alice.

Earl and Franco had gotten to their feet and were staring with disdain at Barry's car.

'We have to ride back in this thing?' questioned Franco.

'It's better than walking,' retorted Alice crossly.

'Only just…,' muttered Earl under his breath.

The two Americans climbed in the back with some difficulty. Franco had to sit with his head tilted to one side, while Earl felt like his backside was being probed again, this time by the springs in the backseat, which were almost poking through the threadbare upholstery. Alice got in the front passenger side. As the car set off and made its way back to Sunderland, they filled Barry in on all the details. Barry almost had a tear in his eye when he heard about the destruction of the fabulous limo.

'Howay, tha's a cryin' shame,' he lamented.

'Don't worry, my friend,' came Earl's voice from the back seat. 'I got two more back at the docks. Always travel with at least three vehicles, ain't that right, Franco?'

'Sure do, boss!'

Barry dropped Earl and Franco back at the docks, next to the gangway to the freighter. They thanked him for coming to get them at such short notice, and Earl promised Barry a ride in one of the other limos to say thank you. Barry was made up.

As the Americans climbed the gangway back onboard the MS Yellow Rose, Barry and Alice set off again in the Montego. Barry dropped Alice at her flat and then headed for home himself.

10.

The day that had been delegated for speeches at The Dockers working men's club had come around, and the evening was due to start at 7pm. Len Finch, as was his custom, had arrived early. So early, in fact, that none of the staff had yet arrived. He let himself in with his own key and sat at a table reading his copy of *The Sunderland Recorder* while he waited. The front headline read:

Crazy American Tourists Cause Gridlock Misery

The paper had gone on to explain how a Texan senator's stretch limousine had blocked a popular holiday route to the Pennines, causing sheer pandemonium in the district. A photo of the limousine dangling over a humpback bridge had been printed underneath.

Mr Finch knew with absolute certainty that there was only one American senator in the vicinity who drove a stretch limo. And that would be the erstwhile mentioned Senator Earl Sanderson III. Len's thin lips curled into a spiteful sneer as he gloated over the story. The senator was due to be making his own speech as the new owner of Sunderland docks tonight. It was promising to be an entertaining evening.

Len was disturbed from his cogitations by the noise of the club's door opening. The barman, Derek Barlow, was coming in to start his shift for the evening. He was a mean, cantankerous individual with a thin, saggy, mirthless face. As he shuffled off behind the bar to set up, he glanced over in Len's direction and greeted him with a frown and a barely discernible nod, which for Derek Barlow was being as friendly as could be.

105

It is an odd phenomenon of life that some people, by a strange quirk of fate, end up working in jobs for which they are wholly unsuitable. And Mr Barlow was certainly a case in point. Derek Barlow should not have been working in the hospitality industry. In fact, he shouldn't have been dealing with the general public at all. And he certainly shouldn't have been working behind a bar. He'd sooner spit in your eye than give you a smile. His idea of customer service was to begrudgingly serve your drinks in as surly a fashion as was humanly possible, with a conversation consisting of harrumphing, informing you bluntly what was owed, and then scowling and tutting irritably if you didn't have the exact amount ready in your hand.

He and Len were friends, or, more accurately, comrades. Len stood up from his table and went over to the bar. He ordered a bottle of brown ale.

'Two fifty,' said Derek with a grimace, slamming a glass on the bar and opening a bottle of ale.

Len had the correct amount in hand, which was duly handed over and thrown grumpily in the till by Derek.

'The Tory woman will be coming in tonight,' Len informed him.

'What of it?' came the terse reply.

'You know what to do?' said Len with a malicious gleam in his eye.

'I do.'

Len returned to his table as the front door opened again. This time a young man strode in holding a large guitar case in one hand and a music stand in the other. As he took in the grim surroundings he shook his head wistfully, making his beaded dreadlocks fly haphazardly around his face. He was a handsome man with finely chiselled features, a warm smile and keen intelligent eyes. His name was Reginald Hill, but

106

everyone knew him as Reggie, and he was the musician booked to play his set before the start of the proceedings for the night. As he set up the music stand and placed the sheet music upon it, he flashed a friendly smile at the other two men in the room but received little acknowledgement in return. Unperturbed, he took out his guitar from its case and began to tune up.

The club slowly began to fill up and Reggie began to play his set. He played a mixture of some local folk songs, some soft rock and roll, and a little reggae. He was going down well with the dockers. None of them had even tried to mash his face in.

The Labour MP, Alan Bailey, was sat quietly in the corner studying the notes for his speech. A short time later, Alice and Barry made an appearance in the doorway. The presence of the new Conservative candidate entering the club was turning a few heads, that was for sure.

Seeing Alan sat in the corner, Barry gave him a wave and led Alice across the barroom to make the introduction. Alice shook Alan's hand and thanked him for his invitation tonight so that she could make a speech of her own. As they chatted, she found him to be a very pleasant, genuine and kind man. She couldn't help but like him, and likewise Alan thought Alice to be a charming, down to earth and honest woman. Not at all what he was expecting. Barry was really pleased to see they were getting on, not least because he and Alan had been good friends for years. They went to watch the football together most Saturday afternoons.

As Alice looked around the room, Barry surreptitiously pointed out Len Finch to her. She tried to catch his eye but he was talking intensely to some of the dock workers, and, it seemed to her, he was resolutely trying to ignore her anyway. Instead, she walked up to the bar to order some drinks. She'd noted nearly everyone in the club was drinking brown ale, and she knew Barry would too, so she decided to try it herself. *When in Rome...and all that*, she thought.

'Yes?' was the blunt remark from the barman as she reached the bar.

'Two brown ales, please,' requested Alice politely.

The grouchy barman regarded her as if she'd just insulted his mother but then turned his back and went off to procure the bottles of ale. He returned and placed them, along with two glasses, on the bar. Alice picked up one of the glasses and poured the ale in. She took it over to hand to Barry who was still chatting with Alan. As she did so, Derek took the other glass and quickly poured a double vodka into the bottom. He then poured the ale in on top.

Alice returned to the bar to find the barman had poured her drink out for her. Perhaps he wasn't such an ogre after all.

'Five pounds,' he snarled.

She handed him a ten-pound note, which he snatched out of her fingers irritably, and then tutted over to the till to ring it in. He returned with her five-pound note in change and placed it deliberately in a pool of beer on the bar top. He immediately turned to serve another customer.

What an obnoxious pratt, she thought to herself as she picked up her soggy change. Her first impression of him had been right after all. She made her way back to Barry and then they found a table of their own to sit at. Alice took a sip of her beer. She thought it tasted a little odd, but she'd never had a brown ale before, so she just assumed that was how it was supposed to be.

Suddenly a hush fell on the room and all eyes turned expectantly to the entrance door as a gargantuan, black-suited giant of a man brushed through the doorway, followed closely by a swaggering fellow all togged up like Buffalo Bill. Everyone knew that this was the new owner of the dockyards.

'What a shit hole!' Earl remarked loudly to his colleague, before realising everyone was watching and listening to him intently.

The pair moved off swiftly towards the bar and the conversation in the room resumed.

Earl strutted up to the bar, where he was confronted by one of the most unwelcoming faces he had ever encountered in his life.

'Yes?' said Derek sourly.

'Howdy partner,' beamed Earl, trying to inject some life into the scene. 'So, what do you recommend to drink in these here parts?'

'Brown ale,' came the dreary reply.

Earl's face fell. He didn't really relish the idea of more warm, flat, fusty-tasting beer right now.

'Say now,' said Earl with an optimism he didn't really feel. 'You wouldn't happen to have any American beer back there, would you, buddy?'

'American beer? Like lager, you mean?'

'If you say so.'

'Might be some in the storeroom out back.'

Earl smiled heartily at the barman, but Derek did not move and just remained standing behind the bar staring eerily at him.

'Well?' urged Earl encouragingly.

'You expect me to fetch some?'

'If it ain't too much trouble,' said Earl sarcastically.

Derek sighed loudly, slowly turned on his heel, and heaved himself off to the storeroom, feigning a painful limp in his left leg for good measure.

'Well, whoopie shit!' Earl exclaimed to Franco, twirling his finger in the air in mock celebration. 'Wasn't that big hearted of him!'

After a minute or two, the barman hobbled back to his position behind the bar, rubbing some dust off several bottles he'd located at the back of the storeroom.

'Found some,' he said, opening two bottles and placing them on the bar for Earl and Franco.

'Why, thank you,' said Earl, taking a chug out of the bottle.

'The lads call that stuff *Sex On The Beach*, you know,' Derek informed him with a sly glance.

Earl swallowed and smiled appreciatively. 'They must think it's real good beer, huh?'

'Not really,' said the barman, snidely. 'They call it that because they reckon it's frigging close to water.'

Derek knew the joke was an adaption of an old *Monty Python* gag, but it certainly worked its charm on the American. Earl's eyes nearly popped out of their sockets. '*What!!*' he shouted over the bar, his blood pressure rising rapidly.

Derek just stared back at him, looking pleased with himself at managing to cause such offence. Franco decided it was time to intervene.

'You want me to whack him, boss?' he asked reaching a huge hand towards Derek's throat.

Suddenly the smirk was falling off Derek's face.

110

But Derek was saved by the bell, or rather, the tapping of a teaspoon against the side of a glass. Alan Bailey was on his feet and was attempting to get everyone's attention for the speeches to begin. Reggie wound up his act and, placing his guitar on a stand, he went and found a seat close to the bar.

'Ladies and gentlemen,' Alan began. 'I'd like to start the evening by introducing to you the new owner of Sunderland docks, Senator Earl Sanderson III.'

He indicated for Earl to stand up and make his presence known to the dockers in attendance. Earl got to his feet, removing his hat as he did so and raised it in his right hand in a gesture of greeting. Franco, meanwhile, positioned just behind him, glared malevolently around the room.

There was a smattering of lacklustre applause.

'And now,' continued Alan, 'I'm sure the new owner would like to take to the stage to say a few words.'

Alan sat back down and waited expectantly as Earl replaced the Stetson on his head and drew himself up to his full height. He then strode confidently across the barroom, his boot spurs chinking, and climbed the few steps onto the stage. He grasped the microphone firmly in his hand.

'You're darn tootin' I do!' he commenced, shouting angrily at the gathered attendees. 'I just paid millions of goddamn dollars to buy this dockyard, and the first thing I know of is that you lazy, limey, sons of bitches immediately stop working and go on strike! Now what in the name of Captain Ahab's harpoon did you do that for!'

Disturbed by this threatening tone of speech, Len Finch was on his feet immediately.

'How dare you speak to us like that!' he fumed. 'You have no respect for the workers! As I suspected!'

There followed a chorus of affronted cheers and hollers from the dockers to back him up.

In response, Earl drew his finger under his chin giving a cutthroat signal to Franco and jerked a thumb towards Mr Finch. The hulking form of Franco strode purposefully across the floor and stopped in front of him. A hand reached out and grasped Len by the front of his jacket and lifted him bodily off the ground. He left him dangling in the air as he turned to his employer.

'You want me to silence him permanently, boss?'

Alan Bailey, horrified, rushed to intervene.

'Put him down, this instant,' he implored Franco. 'Can't you see you're choking him?'

'I'm trying to choke him!' responded Franco candidly.

Some of the dockers were now getting to their feet and, with intent in their eyes, were advancing cautiously towards Franco.

Alice caught Earl's eye and frantically gesticulated at him to make Franco stop. Earl looked disappointed, but he respected Alice's advice, so he called Franco off.

'Let him go,' he ordered the bodyguard.

Franco reluctantly released his grip and Len fell back into his chair, purple-faced and spluttering for breath.

'Now you all listen up!' hollered Earl, giving a beady eye to all the dockers. 'I want you all back at work first thing in the morning. I'm a fair man, and I'll pay you a good wage. And I want these docks to be successful. Goddamn it, I'm even going to be pouring more money and investment into this enterprise! Don't you get it? I'm trying to help you!'

Len Finch had recovered sufficiently to challenge him again.

'You're a monster!' he accused indignantly. 'I will not stand idly by and…'

'You shut your yap!' Earl berated him. Pointing a finger at the dockers, he carried on his remonstration. 'From now on, it's my way or the highway! And woe betide if any one of you crosses me again, because my associate and I will…*kick…your…ass!* Y'hear?'

And with that he beckoned Franco to follow him and the two Americans swept out of the barroom and made their way back to the MS Yellow Rose. The senator was content that he'd got his point across. Albeit none too subtly.

A stunned Alan Bailey was looking shocked and staring goggle-eyed at the door through which the senator and his henchman had just exited. He shook his head in disbelief but then rallied himself as he tried to get on with the next round of speeches.

'Er…,' he said. 'Thank you for those kind words. And now I'd like everyone to put their hands together and give a warm welcome…to Ms Alice Chesham!'

There was another smattering of unenthusiastic applause.

Alice got to her feet and smiled kindly at Alan. 'Thank you,' she mouthed at him.

'Ms Chesham is the new Conservative candidate for the area,' Alan informed the room. 'And I'm sure we're all eager to hear what she has to say. Ms Chesham, please do head up to the stage.'

Alice walked confidently up to the stage, holding her speech ready in her left hand. It was the same one she had given at the polo club. The speech had gone down so well, she thought there was little point in rewriting it.

She began her oration, as before, promising to lobby for more rights for horse riders to use bridleways, byways and permissive tracks. All too often, she told her new audience, these pathways were obstructed or overgrown, making them impossible to ride through on horseback. If she were voted in, she would use all her ministerial powers to ensure better access for equestrian pursuits.

A resounding silence echoed around the barroom. Which was not exactly the reaction she had been hoping for.

Next, she expounded her plans to curb anti-social behaviour by banning hoodies and preventing teenagers from gathering in large intimidating groups. She was also going to crack down on littering, graffiti and fly tipping by introducing hefty fines and forcing those responsible into community service.

As she paused for the applause, a solitary cough could be heard coming from a far corner. She was beginning to get a bit anxious at the lack of response but soldiered on.

Lastly, she was going to shake up the council and ensure that it introduced proper ecological and environmental policies for the protection of the countryside, woodland, marshland and the coastal waters of Sunderland. No more would companies and industries get away with polluting the environment. Not on her watch.

Barry broke into ecstatic applause and tried to get a cheer going from the crowd. But his well-intended endeavour, to coin a phrase, died on its arse. Alice quietly vacated the stage and went back to sit at their table. Barry, feeling she needed some moral support, smiled at her sympathetically.

'Ne'er mind, pet,' he said, holding her hand. 'Ye cannae expect to win forst time, like. Let me get ye anutha drink ter console yersen.'

Alice nodded glumly and Barry went off to the bar to get another round. Len Finch was watching her closely and a thin smirk crossed his lips as he gloated over her miscalculation with undisguised pleasure.

Alan Bailey had now risen from his chair and was making his way up to the small stage. Far livelier applause and cheering greeted him. He began to make his speech. Alice noted his topics included helping those living in poverty with a supply of extra foodbanks, ensuring ongoing facilities at the local hospital, and increasing benefits for those struggling with bills and unemployment.

Alice was kicking herself. How could she have been so stupid to think the issues that were important in her old constituency would be relevant here? Alan's speech was so much better and on-point than her own. She had to concede he knew exactly what he was doing.

Barry had ordered another round of drinks from the miserable Derek. He didn't much want to communicate with him further, so he turned away from the bar to listen to Alan's speech. As he did so, Derek Barlow took the opportunity to spike Alice's glass with another double vodka. He then poured out both beers into the glasses.

'Five pounds,' he barked loudly to get Barry's attention.

Barry gave him a five-pound note and then returned to the table with the drinks. Alice needed a stiffener after her disastrous performance, and she gulped down half the glass of beer to drown her sorrows. As she listened to the remainder of Alan's speech, she started to feel just a tiny bit light-headed and giddy. When Alan was finished, she joined in the clapping and cheers with good grace. Alan acknowledged her praise gratefully. As he went back to his seat, Alice was sure the room began to spin a little.

Alan then announced the final speech of the evening, which was going to be made by the Trades Union boss, Len Finch.

'Oh, God, no!' said Alice a little too loudly. A few people sat nearby craned their heads to stare at her with curious concern. She didn't notice them. She was currently far more interested in her beer glass, which she now drained and banged down on the table clumsily.

Len Finch began his speech by venomously berating the new owner, Earl Sanderson, who, he pointed out, had shown his true colours tonight in no uncertain terms. A hum of general agreement sounded around the room.

But a cry of 'Rubbish!' came from somewhere towards the back.

Len ignored the remark and continued with his criticism of the senator and his violent bodyguard. Len was imploring the dockers to rebel and refuse to go back to work.

'What do you say, comrades?' he asked of them fervently.

Out of the blue, the sound of someone blowing a very long and raucous raspberry could be heard, followed by a rowdy shout of '*Get off!*'

To everyone's surprise the heckling seemed to be coming from the table where the new Conservative candidate and her assistant were sitting. Ms Chesham appeared to be chuckling uncontrollably to herself while swaying gently in her seat. Barry was looking at her with apprehension. This behaviour was definitely out of character for her.

Len Finch couldn't believe his luck. His little plan to get the Tory woman inebriated was working a charm. First, she'd made that God-awful speech and now she was making a total fool of herself to boot. He decided to press home his advantage.

'And look, brothers and sisters, what our friends in the Conservative Party have sent us,' he sneered, pointing a finger in Alice's direction. 'This is the scorn with which they regard us!'

Alice wasn't going to take that lying down. She staggered to her feet and racked her fuddled brains for a brilliantly stinging political putdown.

'*Up yours, Trotsky!*' she slurred magnanimously, and gave him the finger for good measure.

She then slumped back in her chair, and slowly toppled over into Barry's lap, passing out cold.

'Need I say more?' said Len Finch smugly.

The barroom broke out with scornful laughter as Alice lay sprawled out on her assistant's lap, dribbling slightly onto his knee. As Len came down off the stage he was greeted with cheers, applause and shouts of solidarity. He did a round of the barroom, shaking hands with the dockers, and giving his assurance that strike action was the only way forward. He then crossed the floor to depart the club, giving a surreptitious wink to the barman as he passed by. Soon the club began to empty of people until only a handful were left.

Barry was still sat cradling Alice in his arms. He looked very upset and his eyes were red from tears of indignation. He knew something bad had happened to Alice, but he couldn't think how it had been done. Or who could have been low and cruel enough to do it.

Alan Bailey came over with a look of worried concern on his face.

'Is she okay?' he asked apprehensively. 'What happened to her?'

'I dunno,' croaked Barry. 'One minute she wus fine and the next she wus oot of it!'

'I know what happened,' came another voice from behind them.

117

They all turned round to see who had spoken.

Reggie was near the stage packing up his guitar and music gear. He looked at them with a steely glint in his eye.

'Her drinks were spiked,' he told them. 'I saw that vile barman pour something in her beer glass. I wasn't sure what he'd done, but looking at the poor girl now, it's obvious.'

'Are you one hundred percent sure that's what you saw?' questioned Alan.

'Pretty sure, yeah. It wasn't at all righteous, man. It was a wicked thing to do,' replied Reggie.

Alan went over to the bar, where Derek Barlow was still tidying up. He looked up as Alan approached.

'Did you spike Ms Chesham's drink?' he confronted Derek directly.

'Did I do *what*?' retorted Derek.

'You heard. Did you spike her drink?'

'Of course not.'

'I have an eyewitness who says he saw you.'

'Who?'

'Reggie.'

'And you believe that reprobate over me, do you?' spat Derek.

'I ain't no reprobate, man,' said Reggie hotly. 'And I saw what I saw.'

'No one will take your word over mine,' Derek told him brusquely.

'Why's that? Because I'm black? Is that it?' Reggie rounded on him furiously.

Derek stared back defiantly but said nothing.

'When Ms Chesham recovers, I'll be asking her to press charges,' Alan informed him.

Derek snapped.

'*Get out of here!*' he yelled at them over the bar. 'Now!'

Barry picked Alice up in his arms and carried her outside. Alan and Reggie followed directly behind. Once they were outside, Alan started the conversation again.

'You'd be willing to testify?' he asked Reggie.

'With pleasure, man,' replied Reggie. 'That guy is a real creep.'

'I've never liked him either,' admitted Alan.

Barry opened the back door of his Montego and lay Alice on the backseat.

'I'm gannae tek her back to her flat,' he told them, 'but I'm wurried aboot her, like, in the state she's in. She shuldna be on her oon. But I've gorra work in the mornin' so I cannae really dee it. Can either of yee lads help us oot?'

'I've got to work too, Barry,' lamented Alan. 'Sorry, pal.'

'Reggie? How aboot ye?'

'Sure, Barry, I can take care of her,' Reggie said. 'I've got to go to college tomorrow afternoon, but I can stay with her until then. No problem.'

'Oh, magic, son,' sighed Barry in relief. 'Yer a star. Well, jump in te car, an we'll get her back herm safe 'n' sound.'

They bid Alan goodnight, promising to take this matter up again in the morning. Then Barry and Reggie got in the Montego and drove Alice back to her flat. Reggie helped Barry get her onto her bed, where they removed her shoes and placed the covers over her. Barry disappeared off home, and Reggie made himself as comfortable as he could on the sofa. Her bedroom door had been left open so he could hear her breathing softly and would know she was all right.

*

Back in the working men's club, Derek rang Len Finch's mobile phone number, hoping to catch him before he went to bed.

'Yes?' said Len, answering his phone on the fourth ring. He'd recognised the number as being the club's.

'They're onto us,' Derek reported.

'What do you mean?' Len queried.

'I was seen spiking her drink. The guitarist boy, Reggie. He says he saw me.'

'Blast it!' cursed Len.

He had to think of a way to stay ahead of the game. The solution came to him directly.

'Derek, I need you to do something for me…,' he said slyly.

After Len had hung up, Derek finished tidying up and restocking the bar and then sat at one of the tables to pen a letter. The letter was sealed in an envelope and left on the bar counter marked *To Whom It May Concern.* Derek then turned off all the lights, locked up and walked the short distance round the corner back to his small, terraced house.

The letter contained his notice of resignation, due to alleged ill health. Len Finch had instructed him to do so, on the promise that he'd give him another job working for him at the trade union. But with Derek effectively removed from the proceedings, he was sure no one would pursue the matter further, and his own involvement in the whole tawdry affair would remain a secret.

11.

After a fitful night's sleep Alice awoke to the sound of a kettle being boiled and someone rattling around with crockery and cutlery. Her head was pounding and her mouth was as dry as the Gobi desert.

She realised she was in her own bed, although she seemed to be still wearing her business suit. *What the hell happened last night?* she wondered. The last thing she remembered was applauding Alan Bailey's speech.

She sensed someone enter the room and listened to them gently open the curtains. The bright sunlight hurt her eyes, even though they were still firmly screwed shut. She really needed to know who the person might be, so, slowly and tentatively, she opened her eyes slightly and took a peek.

A handsome, smiling face of a young man was hovering over her. Beaded dreadlocks were hanging down round his neck. His dark brown eyes were full of concern as he looked down benevolently at her. She recognised him as the guitar player from last night.

'Good morning,' Reggie said softly. 'How are you doing?'

'I've felt better,' Alice replied honestly.

'You had a rough night,' Reggie told her. 'Would you like a cup of herbal tea? I found some chamomile in your cupboard.'

'That would be lovely.' She nodded her head eagerly, immediately regretting the movement as it set off an explosion of painful fireworks in her brain. 'Ouch!' she cried.

'I'll see if I can find some painkillers too,' he said and disappeared into the kitchen.

What was he doing in my flat? she pondered. *Did I invite him back?* She couldn't remember.

Reggie came back into the bedroom with the tea, a glass of orange juice and a packet of paracetamol. He set it all down on the bedside table and then sat in an armchair next to the window. Alice drank some of the juice and washed down some painkillers with it. She then sat up in bed and sipped her chamomile while regarding Reggie furtively.

'Erm...,' she began. 'Oh, I'm sorry, I don't even know your name.'

'It's Reggie,' he informed her. 'Reggie Hill.'

'Reggie, I'm just wondering why you are in my flat...did I...I mean, did we, er...you know...?'

Reggie grinned mischievously.

'Don't worry,' he assured her. 'Your honour is intact! I was here last night to look after you. That's all. Barry asked me if I could stay with you. He was worried after you got spiked...'

'I got spiked?'

'Yes, I'm sorry to say you did.'

'But how?'

'The barman. I think I saw him do it. He's a real jerk.'

'Yes, he was. I remember. But why would he do that to me?'

123

'I think he wanted to get you drunk so you'd make a mistake,' Reggie suggested.

'Well, thank goodness I didn't do anything embarrassing or silly,' Alice remarked.

A pregnant pause in the conversation hung in the room.

'Er...well,' stuttered Reggie uncomfortably.

'Er...well? That doesn't sound too good. Come on...tell me. What did I do?'

'Oh, nothing much.'

'Tell me!'

'You just gave someone the bird, that's all.'

'Oh...I did? Who?'

'Len Finch.'

'Oh, God!'

'And you might have called him Trotsky.'

'Oh, God!'

'And then you may have fallen over and passed out...a bit.'

'Oh, God!'

'I doubt anyone even noticed,' said Reggie, trying to downplay the fiasco.

'Just the whole club, right?'

'Well...maybe,' conceded Reggie.

Alice put her tea down on the bedside table and hung her head in her hands. Her shoulders began to gently shake as she started to sob openly. Hot tears of shame ran down her face. Reggie moved over from the armchair and sat on the side of the bed. He put his arms round her shoulders and held her gently until her sobs subsided slightly.

'It's okay,' he soothed her. 'Don't worry. Everything will be all right.'

'Oh, Reggie, how can it?' she wailed. 'I've made a right mess of it. Father would have been better off sending Alfie.'

'Who's Alfie?' asked Reggie.

'He's just my loopy little brother,' sighed Alice.

'Oh,' said Reggie, not really understanding. 'You want me to phone him?'

'Oh no, no. It wouldn't help. But whatever am I going to do?' wailed Alice. 'No one's going to take me seriously now.'

'Now listen up. Last night wasn't your fault,' Reggie soothed her. 'I know everyone around here and I'm going to make sure they all know the truth of what happened last night. So don't you worry.'

'You'd do that for me?' asked Alice incredulously.

'Of course!' said Reggie firmly. 'I'm not going to let that Derek Barlow get away with it.'

'Thank you, Reggie,' Alice smiled, starting to feel a little better.

Alice and Reggie chatted together for the rest of the morning. Alice told him about her family background and longstanding roots in Norfolk and her political aspirations. In response, Reggie informed her about his own life story. It was tinged with sadness.

Reggie had been orphaned at the age of fourteen. His father had been a teacher from the former British colony of

Southern Cameroons (Ambazonia) in Central Africa. He'd had to flee to Britain in 1990 to escape the economic and political crises affecting his homeland at the time. His mother's family had been from Antigua and they had emigrated to Britain during the Windrush years. Her family had settled in the North East. The two had met while working at the same school in Newcastle. In 2017, Reggie's father and mother had travelled to Cameroon to join the protests to protect the Southern Cameroons from being forcibly assimilated from British-based judicial and educational systems to French-based ones. The government had dealt with the protests violently and in the ensuing bloody conflict, both of his parents had been tragically killed.

Following his terrible loss, Reggie had subsequently been raised by his grandmother on his mother's side. He'd taken on her surname of Hill. Her first name was Lilly and she was a tough but loving woman. It had been hard for her to raise Reggie on her own, but she'd done her best to bring him up well. A task she'd accomplished exemplarily. She lived in Sunderland, not far from the docks. Reggie promised Alice that he would introduce her to his grandmother very soon.

Their conversation was interrupted at lunchtime by the ringing of the doorbell. Reggie went to see who it was. He came back into the bedroom with Barry and Alan in tow. Between them, they'd decided to pay a visit to Alice's flat on their lunchbreak to check on her. They'd driven over in Barry's Montego.

'How're ye deein, pet?' enquired Barry with genuine concern.

'I'm fine, Barry, thank you,' replied Alice. 'You left me in good hands.'

'Aye, ees a canny lad is oor Reggie,' beamed Barry.

'I'm so glad you're recovering well,' added Alan. 'We were all very concerned. It was disgraceful what happened to you.'

'Thank you, Alan,' said Alice sincerely.

'Did you find out any more about that worm, Derek Barlow?' asked Reggie.

'Yes. I went down to the Dockers club just before we came over here and I found this laying on the bar counter,' said Alan, producing an envelope from his coat pocket and showing them Derek's letter of resignation. 'I was going to demand he be fired from his job forthwith, but as you can see, he's resigned.'

'Maybe he felt ashamed,' suggested Reggie, 'and done the decent thing by quitting.'

'Ah doot it,' said Barry. 'That slimy shite hasna any decency at url.'

'I agree,' concurred Alan. 'It's all very fishy. But there's not much else we can do about it now. The rug has been pulled from under our feet, so to speak.'

'What's going to happen with the club now then?' queried Reggie. 'Who's going to run it now that Barlow's gone?'

'Good question,' said Alan, giving it some thought. 'I think the club is owned by the dockyard. So, logically, Senator Sanderson is now the new proprietor. He probably doesn't even know.'

'Man, I'd love to get my hands on the Dockers club…,' Reggie murmured in contemplation.

'What?' said Alan in surprise. 'Really? You'd be interested in taking over the running of the club?'

'Yeah,' nodded Reggie. 'Too right. I reckon I could really turn it round. I've always dreamed of running my own venue. I'd love it.'

'I'm on good terms with the senator,' put in Alice. 'I can ask him if you like.'

'Wow! You'd do that for me?' exclaimed Reggie.

'One good turn deserves another,' smiled Alice. 'I'll call him this afternoon.'

Reggie beamed.

'Well, that's that sorted, then,' enthused Alan. 'and now I suggest we leave the lady in peace. Come on, lads.'

The men bade their farewells to Alice and started towards the door.

'Can you give me a lift to my afternoon class at the college, Barry?' asked Reggie.

'Aye. Nay wurries, pal. Wha' ur ye studying anyway, these days?'

'Literature and poetry.'

'Oh, canny. Which poets, like?'

'The Irish poets. Russel, Boland, Yeats, Montague, Beckett, Joyce to name a few,' replied Reggie, surprised at Barry's hitherto undiscovered interest in the arts.

'Oh aye, the Irish poets,' said Barry knowledgeably. 'Ye cannae beat a good Limerick can ye?'

As Alice showed them to the door, she shared a secret chuckle with Alan and Reggie over Barry's comments. She closed the door behind them.

God bless Barry Higgins, reflected Alice. He never failed to cheer her up. In fact, her spirits had been lifted considerably by *all* her new friends. *By hook or by crook*, she resolved, *I am going to get back on my feet.*

128

12.

Later that afternoon, after Alice had showered and freshened
up and was feeling almost human again, she'd telephoned
home. Her mother had answered the call and Alice had poured
her heart out to her. As mothers do, Henrietta had listened to
her woes diligently. She had sensed her daughter could use a
little help, so she'd come up with the idea of inviting Senator
Sanderson and his associate, Franco Gambini, to be their
guests at Chesham Manor for a day or so. They'd really lay on
the hospitality and ensure the Americans were well and truly
buttered up, to secure a firm friendly relationship between
them. If they managed to help the senator's takeover of the
docks to be successful, it would bode well for Alice's own
political interests. Henrietta had told her she would talk it over
with Humphrey and Carstairs and get everything arranged.
She'd instructed Alice to invite them over the following
weekend. And, of course, she was welcome to invite any other
of her new friends along too.

     As soon as Henrietta had hung up, Alice placed a call
to the senator and made the proposal. The senator had been
delighted to accept. He'd even offered to drive them all down
to Norfolk in his second limousine, Earl II, which had just
been rolled out from its shipping container. The senator had
insisted that Barry join them for the trip, as he wanted to repay
him for picking them up after the disastrous humpback bridge
incident. Alice had assured him that Barry would be thrilled at
the opportunity to join them and ride in the stretch limo.

     While she had Earl on the line, she had informed him
about the goings on with the Dockers club management. He
had been surprised to discover that he owned the club and had

immediately pledged a large sum of money to refurbish the place. Alice had taken the opportunity to put in a good word for Reggie to take over after Derek Barlow's resignation. Earl had told her that if she was recommending him, then that was all the endorsement he needed to give Reggie the job. The senator had said he could hardly be worse than the surly Barlow. Alice had wholeheartedly agreed. The senator had requested that Reggie come along for the weekend too, so that he might get to know him better. Alice had been delighted. She'd really wanted Reggie to come along too.

*

Len Finch was sat at his desk at the Trade Union office. Following his run in with the new owner of Sunderland docks at the speech night, Len was all the more determined to keep the strike going and the docks closed. He was going to teach that God-awful American capitalist pig a thing or two about the power of the unions.

To show his appreciation to his comrade Derek, who had selflessly sacrificed his job to further the cause, Mr Finch had appointed him the position of being his personal and loyal assistant. Len knew too, that with Barlow having few moral qualms, he could be relied upon to do his dirty work should the need arise.

As the days passed by with no activity at the docks, Senator Earl Sanderson III was getting angrier and angrier, and Len Finch was getting smugger and smugger.

*

In the constituency of North Norfolk, the Honourable Member of Parliament Mr Alfred Chesham was having some problems of his own. His father, along with the Chancellor of the Duchy of Lancaster, had, in their infinite wisdom, decided that Alfie needed "an agenda".

Thus far, Alfie had survived in the brutal world of politics by looking smarmy in his natty suit, keeping his trap shut, and doing only what his father or Carstairs advised him to. But this was deemed insufficient for a working MP, and now the powers that be were demanding more of him.

The agenda that had been unceremoniously thrust upon him and that he was now purportedly the Conservative expert upon, was the tricky business of offshore tax havens. And namely, his being put in charge of shutting them down. A subject Alfie knew precisely nothing about. He didn't really even understand what they were, despite Carstairs' best endeavours to explain the thorny issue to him.

After a week of tutelage on the matter, Alfie had had to present himself in front of the press to explain how his department intended to deal with the problem. Carstairs had provided him with the speech to read out. It had sensibly been agreed previously that Carstairs would write it. This was due to Alfred's own grammar being so poor that he genuinely didn't know a colon from his arse.

The speech had gone as well as could be expected. Alfred had explained to the room that many of the tax havens were self-governing islands based in the Mediterranean, Caribbean or even further afield. It was these that Alfred and his department would be dealing with forthwith.

It was when he had reached the end of the speech, when the floor had been opened for a question-and-answer session, that young Alfred had suffered a bit of a hiccup. A left-wing tabloid journalist, well known for being a wiseacre and all-round troublemaker, had asked him which islands in particular he would be dealing with. Alfred had consulted his notes only to find them somewhat lacking in the finer detail. The journalist had smelt blood and had pounced.

'The Virgin Islands, Gibraltar and The Turks and Caicos are all well-known tax havens,' the journalist proclaimed. Alfie nodded sagely in agreement. 'But,' he continued, 'what about the South Pacific? Would the government, for example, also be tackling the infamous administration on Tracy Island?'

Alfred had never heard of the place but assured him it would be top of the list. There were a few snickers of laughter heard from around the room.

'Excellent news,' declared the journalist. 'And would the Honourable MP agree that the governance of Tracy Island was merely a puppet regime?'

Alfred had wholeheartedly concurred. More laughter could be heard, and now other journalists wanted a piece of the action.

'Isn't it about time the government started to pull some strings behind the scenes?' asked one.

'And what of the reports of unlicensed rocket launches and strange submarine sightings?' asked another.

'Isn't it about time the dictator Jeff Tracy and his family were brought to justice?' demanded another.

Alfred was flummoxed. He had no idea what they were talking about. He merely stood by the podium opening and closing his mouth like a floundering guppy. Not for the first time, he wished his sister would come back and take over her old job.

As the presentation was looking likely to descend into total chaos, Carstairs had saved the day by ringing Alfie's mobile phone and then whisking him off the stage in the pretence that the call was extremely urgent. Once they were safely off stage, Carstairs had explained to him that Tracy

Island was a fictional location from the popular 1960s children's show *Thunderbirds*. The reporter had been pulling his leg and essentially making him look a proper Charlie.

Alfie had groaned inwardly and realised that his bluff had finally been called out. He knew the next day that his face would be splashed across all the newspapers, and that they'd have a field day making him look like a complete and utter incompetent ignoramus. Which, he reluctantly had to admit, was not too far off the mark.

*

Reggie had taken Alice under his wing as far as getting to know the real lives of everyday people living in the poorer areas of Sunderland. Reggie knew a lot of families and had a lot of friends who lived in the area near the docks. Talking to folk door to door in the area had opened Alice's eyes to what issues were important to the local inhabitants. Alice was fast learning that this was a world away from the lives of people in her old constituency.

She was very grateful to Reggie for taking the time to help her. She'd never met a man like Reggie before. Of course, she'd had many a suitor back in Norfolk, but she'd always found the Polo Club 'rich boy' types to be either pretentious, narcissistic or just plain arrogant. Most were only interested in themselves or what others could do for them. She knew none of them would have helped her out so selflessly as Reggie had. And she knew Reggie expected nothing in return. The notion of reward wouldn't even have occurred to him. He was just a good, decent and honourable lad.

One day, as promised, he'd taken her to meet his grandmother, Lilly, at her house near the docks. The house was a two bedroomed terrace. Lilly had one room, and Reggie the other. Reggie had shown Alice around, which had taken less than two minutes. The house was modest and small but well maintained. It had a lovely, homely feel to it. Alice had immediately taken to Lilly. She was a short but stocky lady, and although her face was lined with wrinkles from living a tough life, it was habitually lit up with a warm smile. She had the most jolly and raucous laugh that Alice had ever heard and the Caribbean lilt from her accent lent her an extra charm. Alice could have listened to her all day. When they were saying their goodbyes, Lilly had hugged Alice so hard that she nearly squeezed the life out of her. She'd made Alice promise to come back and visit again soon. Alice had been only too happy to accept the invitation.

*

Humphrey and Henrietta had been busy planning for the upcoming visit of Senator Sanderson. They'd been drawing up an impressive guest list to include local dignitaries, famous artists, a few celebrities and even minor royalty.

Henrietta had of course invited her sister, Baroness Harriet Billingbrooke, to also attend. Due to the relative short notice of the invitation, Harriet had got her knickers in a twist because she couldn't find anyone she trusted to look after Galore, her precious Persian pussycat. Henrietta had told her she'd just have to bring the wretched thing with her if she was that bothered about it. Harriet had agreed she would do just that. She wasn't about to leave Pussy Galore in the hands of anyone she hadn't personally and thoroughly vetted.

Carstairs had been instructed to come up with a classic "British themed" menu with which they hoped to impress the Americans. True to form, the butler had compiled a thoroughly traditional culinary masterpiece, which he was going to prepare, cook and serve himself. The formal dining room was to be set up using the finest antique cutlery, crockery and glassware the Cheshams had in their possession.

To add a little more historic authenticity to the evening, they were also planning to lower the medieval drawbridge and have the senator drive over the moat to be formally welcomed to Chesham Manor. Henrietta had planned a gala champagne reception in the formal gardens. To spice things up further, she had arranged for an impressive firework display to be set up as a surprise. The pyrotechnics were to be concealed in the ha-ha at the end of the paddock so the guests would be unaware of their presence.

It was all looking set to be an extremely momentous event.

*

The Dockers club had been undergoing some major refurbishment thanks to the injection of cash supplied by Earl Sanderson III. He'd donated over £50,000. Reggie had been delighted and soon got busy supervising the refurbishments.

They'd ripped out the old carpet and replaced it with a new wood effect floor. The old tables and chairs had been thrown out and replaced with much more comfortable seating. The lighting had been upgraded with spotlights and mood lighting. The toilet facilities had been refitted with new, modern sanitary ware, and fresh tiling. New lighting had been installed in the toilets and hallway too. The bar counter had been sanded back and revarnished with a much lighter shade of wood stain, which brightened the whole bar area up. Trendy neon lights had been fitted behind the bar along with some more mood lighting. The small stage area had also been improved with better lighting and a whole new state-of-the-art PA system. Lastly, the windows had been replaced with modern insulated UPVC, the whole exterior of the building had been repainted, and a new "The Dockers" sign had been erected on the wall, with floodlights lighting up the scene during the night-time.

Reggie had asked for Alice's help with some of the interior design. He acknowledged a woman's touch for the softer furnishings and decoration would be very beneficial. They'd both helped out with the decorating by painting the walls and ceilings and cutting in around the edges. Alice had also picked out some fabulous artwork prints to hang on the walls, which give the club a real contemporary buzz.

All in all, The Dockers had been transformed from a dreary old man's boozer to a modern, welcoming, comfortable bar. Reggie was made up. He was ecstatic about the renovations and being put in charge of the club. He was eternally grateful to Alice for her help in recommending him to Senator Sanderson and for assisting him with the upgrading of the bar. When they'd finally finished the last of the painting, he'd given Alice a warm embrace, and moved to give her a friendly kiss on her cheek. Reggie's exuberant embrace had caught her unawares and accidentally made her jump, so that her head turned slightly, and the kiss intended for her cheek landed plumb on her mouth.

'I'm so sorry,' Reggie garbled an apology, 'I was just trying to kiss your cheek. I'm sorry…'

Alice fixed him with a warm look straight into his eyes.

'Don't be,' she murmured and leant forward to kiss him back, full on the lips.

The two embraced and kissed for a further whole minute, before parting, gasping for breath. They were both amazed at the strength of their mutual passion.

When Reggie had then asked her if he could start dating her formally, she'd gone weak at the knees. She'd always thought the expression was an exaggeration but now knew better. Alice happily agreed and the two of them, giddy as school children, began to fall in love.

13.

The weekend of the gala event due to take place at Chesham Manor had come around. The event was being held in honour of Senator Earl Sanderson III and everything was ready for the big day.

On the Sunderland docks quayside, Franco was fussing around the huge stretch limousine, Earl II, giving the gleaming paintwork a final polish here and there, and fixing some American flags onto the huge front grille of the car either side of the massive buffalo horns. Everything was prepped and ready for the trip down to Norfolk.

Barry, Alice and Reggie were standing by the side of the car, dressed up in their finest attire, waiting for the senator to appear on the gangway of his freighter. Presently, the sound of booted footsteps accompanied by the chink of brass spurs could be heard coming from the interior of the ship. Soon enough the figure of Earl Sanderson appeared at the top of the gangway bedecked in one of his finest Texan style suits.

'Howdy!' he greeted them as he strode down the gangway. 'I tell you what. I'll ride upfront with Franco and you can all ride together in the saloon. That way you can really spread out and enjoy yourselves. How's that?' He grinned broadly at them with his gleaming white teeth.

'Terrific!' replied Alice.

'Thanks,' added Reggie.

'Bloomin' champion!' enthused Barry, who was so excited at the prospect of riding in the limo that he was now

138

hopping from one foot to the other in excited anticipation. He was trying to spy through the darkened windows, but he couldn't see anything through the obscure glass.

Franco clicked the key fob and the limo doors unlocked. Earl indicated for them to climb inside. Barry was first in and immediately began playing with all the switches and gadgets that were festooned inside. He was like a kid in a candy store.

Alice and Reggie followed him inside, while Earl let himself into the luxurious front passenger seat. Franco put all their luggage into the cavernous boot and then sank himself into the comfortable driver's seat. He set the sat-nav to the address Alice had given him. He'd made sure the route avoided any humpback bridges. The limousine pulled slowly away from the quayside and set off for the journey down to Norfolk.

*

A few hours later the guests were starting to arrive at Chesham Manor. Everyone had crossed the drawbridge over the moat and parked up in the courtyard beyond the main entrance of the manor. Humphrey, Henrietta, Carstairs, Harriet, Alfie and all the other assembled guests were gathered at the far end of the drawbridge, next to the main grand entranceway to Chesham Manor. They were waiting for Senator Sanderson's limousine to arrive so that they could give him a rousing cheer as he drove by. Harriet had even brought Galore along. The graceful Persian cat was draped over her left arm and she was stroking her head gently with her right hand. The cat purred contentedly.

*

139

At 7:25pm, the limousine was cruising steadily through the glorious North Norfolk countryside. They were only a few minutes away from their destination, and they were right on time to arrive precisely at 7:30.

The huge stone and flint entrance pillars which marked the entrance to Chesham Manor came into view and the limousine turned off the main road and onto the long sweeping driveway which led down to the property. Franco and Earl could see the vast manor situated at the end of the drive. It looked truly grandiose and the Americans were duly impressed.

As they drew nearer, they could see the drawbridge and the main entrance, and a large gathering of people waiting on the far side. As they approached, the crowd began to applaud and whistle and cheer enthusiastically. Earl's face broke into a happy smile and, not to be outdone, he wound down the electric window and began to holler 'Yee-haa!' loudly out of the passenger side of the car. Then, he reached inside his jacket and produced his trademark revolver from its holster. Sticking his arm out of the window, he began firing the toy gun randomly and enthusiastically into the air. As the limousine reached the drawbridge, Franco added to the revelry by pressing the horn, causing the *Star-Spangled Banner* to be blared out at a deafening volume.

Galore had been enjoying a peaceful snooze in her owner's arms, when her slumber was rudely and violently brought to an end by a huge cacophony of clapping, whistling, whooping and hollering, followed curtly by thunderous gunshots and an ear-splitting volley from a car horn.

Petrified out of her wits, the cat sprang out of Harriet's arms and in a frenzy of fear and panic, she shot off across the drawbridge, straight into the path of the oncoming limousine.

As they crossed the drawbridge, Earl saw the cat at the last moment as it ran out directly in front of the car. Acting on impulse, he instinctively leant over and grabbed the steering wheel from the surprised Franco and yanked it over to the right in a desperate bid to avoid an accident.

The limousine veered crazily off to the right, slewing sideways, and before they knew it, it had pitched wildly over the side of the drawbridge, flown several feet through the air, and then lugubriously splashed down into the centre of the moat with an almighty kersplosh of water and waves. The limousine slowly sank into the murky waters of the moat almost up to the roof line. The engine duly flooded and stopped running. There was a stunned silence. And then a furious tirade could be heard coming from within the submerged vehicle.

'What in the name of Salome's Seven Veils did you do that for?' roared Earl from beneath the waves.

'What do you mean, boss?' Franco could be heard protesting. 'You was the one who grabbed the wheel!'

Presently, the sunroof hatch on top of the car was slid back and a cowboy hat appeared from the gloom, followed by the irate head of Senator Earl Sanderson III.

'Whose goddamn cat was that?' he demanded angrily.

'How dare you take that tone with me!' the haughty voice of Baroness Harriet Billingbrooke berated him in return. She'd located the frightened Galore and was clutching the cat to her bosom. Harriet's face was a picture of dignified affront.

'Ma'am, you just wrecked my limousine!' Earl bawled at her.

Baroness Billingbrooke drew herself to her full height in indignation.

141

'And you nearly squashed my pussy!' she shouted back ferociously, before realising she'd just made the most dreadful double-entendre, the likes of which even Mrs Slocombe might have baulked at.

The slanging match was suspended temporarily as a rescue bid was made.

A long ladder had been hastily procured and was stretched out from the bankside to reach the top of the limousine. The senator grabbed the end and, climbing out of the sunroof, he made his way unsteadily across the ladder to the safety of the bank. One by one, the other occupants of the wrecked vehicle emerged from the sunroof and eventually all made their way across to the bankside.

While Alice and Reggie looked physically shocked by the accident, Barry was far more upset by the loss of the beautiful limousine. One minute, he'd been lounging on the luxurious leather seats, happily tinkering with all the on-board switches and helping himself to drinks from Earl's cocktail cabinet, and the next minute he was at the bottom of a moat watching the fish swim by.

Franco and Earl seemed less perturbed about the loss of the vehicle, and more annoyed that their flamboyant entrance had gone pear-shaped. Humphrey and Henrietta hastily made their way over to them to make sure no one was injured. Once they'd concluded that everyone was in one piece, they quickly moved the group onwards, through the grand entrance gate and into the formal gardens. Carstairs was ready with the drinks tray, and the gracious hosts carried on with the party, brushing aside the fact they now had a stretch limo at the bottom of their moat as if it were an everyday occurrence.

While dusk drew in, champagne and canapes were served, and the Americans were formally introduced by Lord and Lady Chesham to some of the other distinguished guests. The Mayor of King's Lynn was the first in line, followed by several high-ranking clergy from Walsingham, and lastly, some good friends of Humphrey and Henrietta who happened to be minor royalty. The Americans were politely ushered up in front of them.

'Senator Sanderson, may I have the pleasure to present to you…,' proclaimed Humphrey with much pomposity, 'Earl and Countess Forsyth of Norfolk.'

'Mighty glad to make your acquaintance,' beamed the senator, shaking the proffered hand heartily. 'It sure is great to meet a fellow who shares my name.'

Countess Forsyth pulled a face as though she'd just been slapped with a kipper. 'Dear God, man,' she explained.' He's not *called* Earl…*he is an Earl!*'

'Oh…,' stated the senator blankly, failing to grasp the difference. 'That's neat.'

'Quite…,' intoned the Earl of Norfolk.

'Goodness, is that the time!' Henrietta intervened tactfully. 'It's almost time for our little surprise.'

She hastily chaperoned the Americans further off into the garden, where a large round patio was located in the centre of the lawn. Humphrey followed closely behind. There were several groups of people already situated on the patio, including Alice, Reggie, Barry, Alfie and Aunt Harri. Earlier, Harriet had taken her frightened cat, Galore, indoors and put her in her bedroom to save her from any further upset. Harriet had then returned to rejoin the party. They were all waiting expectantly on the patio for the show to begin.

Presently some dramatic classical music began playing from a hidden outdoor speaker and the magnificent surprise firework display began.

Aunt Harri did love a good firework display. She'd just enjoyed the first rockets going off and was staring excitedly into the night sky, when quite unexpectedly two

143

huge lumbering brutes were suddenly positioned directly in front of her, completely blocking her view.

How bloody rude, she fumed to herself. Well, she wasn't going to stand for that. Reaching for her sturdy umbrella, she grasped the handle and hefted the umbrella upright so that it was shoulder height to the largest of the two lumps standing in front of her. In no uncertain terms the umbrella was rapped sternly several times onto the right shoulder of the mountainous bodyguard all dressed in black. The huge figure began to slowly turn towards her.

Standing beside Harriet, Lord Humphrey Chesham was observing the scene unfolding before him in utmost horror. He was terrified of the senator's sinister looking associate. *This is it*, he thought. *We're all going to be horribly murdered*. Humphrey's life flashed before his eyes, nearly boring him to death.

Franco lugubriously turned his head and craned his neck so that he could see behind him. A frosty, ferocious looking woman in a three-piece suit was glowering up at him.

'Yeah?' he growled menacingly.

'I…Can't…See…Through…Your…Thick…Head,' she informed him, hammering the umbrella onto his shoulder to emphasise each syllable.

Humphrey began shaking in fear uncontrollably. He was certain Harriet had finally taken leave of her senses. Henrietta, observing him with concern, was sure he was having a nervous breakdown.

Senator Sanderson, now joining the fray, turned to look inquisitively at Henrietta. He jerked his thumb in Aunt Harri's direction.

'Who *is* this crazy broad?' he asked bluntly.

'That *crazy broad* is Baroness Harriet Billingbrooke,' replied Henrietta caustically. 'She also happens to be my sister.'

'Oh right,' said Earl awkwardly and smiled ingratiatingly at Aunt Harri. 'So, what can we do for you, ma'am?'

'Go and stand at the back, of course,' snapped the Baroness. 'And remove that silly great hat while you're about it!'

The two Americans stared at her in utter disbelief.

'Come again?' tried Earl.

'You heard! Go on! To the back with the pair of you!'

She brandished her umbrella at them threateningly.

Earl and Franco stood looking dumbly back at her. Never in their lives had they encountered a person such as Baroness Billingbrooke. There was something about her, a sort of inert but powerful authority, that seemed to compel them to obey. As she continued to bore her eyes into them, they felt strangely obliged to do her bidding. Their feet seemed to move of their own accord and the two men slouched off to stand some way behind her. Humphrey scuttled off after them, expounding his apologies. Earl was still staring at Baroness Harriet Billingbrooke in shocked, but reverential, awe. It was his first encounter with a Great British battleaxe, and she'd had a profound effect upon him.

Aunt Harri caught him goggling at her and, smirking happily to herself, she resumed watching the firework display.

Henrietta, miffed at her stroppy sister's behaviour, went to stand at her side. She leant to whisper in her ear.

'Do you have to be quite so Draconian to our guests?' she seethed.

Harriet merely looked at her in surprise. 'They were in my way,' she stated, as if this exonerated her from any wrongdoing.

'Well, for Alice's sake, do you think you could try being a little more becoming?'

'I could, I suppose,' she said coolly.

'Most kind,' said Henrietta sarcastically.

She then went over to join her husband in continuing to woo the senator and his associate. It was almost time to go through for dinner. She was confident the butler's culinary skills would save the day.

*

Carstairs was standing next to the grand ornate patio doors which led from the garden into the dining room. Next to him was a large gong which he'd wheeled out on a serving trolley. The gong had never actually been used before, and was really only for show, but Henrietta thought it would be an impressive way for the butler to announce that dinner was served. Carstairs struck the gong with a hefty felt-covered mallet and a most satisfying metallic bong resonated around the formal grounds.

'My lords, ladies and gentlemen,' he chanted. 'If I may crave your indulgence, your presence is awaited in the dining room.'

Alfie had been chatting with Barry and Reggie on the patio. He'd been getting on well with them. Alice had told him that Reggie was a musician. Alfie had dabbled with electric guitar when he was a teenager. He'd shown some proficiency on the instrument but, typically for Alfie, had given up after a year or so. Reggie, happy that they both had an interest in guitar, had offered to give him a few lessons and tips. Alfie was made up.

When the gong was sounded, Barry and Reggie, unaware of the significance, both looked at Alfie with puzzled expressions.

'Grub's up!' explained Alfie.

They nodded and smiled their understanding and moved off towards the patio door. The various other groups followed suit.

As they entered the dining room, Carstairs showed the assembled guests to their places around the huge rectangular dining table. Senator Sanderson, as guest of honour, was seated at one end, at the head of the table. Either side of him were Alice and Franco. Next to them were Reggie and Alfie and then Aunt Harri and Barry. In the centre of the table, sitting opposite each other, were the Earl and Countess of Norfolk. Then there were the various clergy, the Mayor of King's Lynn, and a few noted locals. Finally, at the far end of the table sat Humphrey and Henrietta.

When all the guests were seated, Carstairs began the proceedings by doing a round of the table serving the wine. And brown ale.

'Howay, tha's champion!' Barry thanked the butler and happily began chugging his beer.

The Countess of Norfolk, sipping her white wine, raised an eyebrow at him.

Barry responded as only Barry could. 'Bottoms up!' he declared gleefully, clinking her wine glass with his pint mug.

Alice noted that the conversation around the table was a little stilted. The Americans hadn't said a word, the clergy might as well have taken a vow of silence, and even

Aunt Harri was being uncharacteristically circumspect. She hoped dearly that someone would break the ice soon.

The Earl of Norfolk, almost as if sensing her wishes, decided he'd try and strike up a conversation with the cheery, beer swilling fellow who was currently appalling his wife. Using one of his stock lines when meeting members of the general public, he cleared his throat and fixed Barry in his gaze.

'And are you going anywhere nice for your holidays this summer?' he asked half-heartedly.

Barry was taken a little by surprise that an actual, real Earl was attempting to make conversation with him. But he swiftly pulled himself together.

'Oh, aye,' he replied. 'I'm actually thinkin' of gan on safari, as it 'appens.'

The surprising response had garnered the attention of the whole table. All heads turned their way.

The Earl of Norfolk was in his element. He'd been on many a safari in his lifetime.

'Oh, how wonderful,' he enthused. 'Whereabouts? South Africa? Namibia? Kenya? The Massai Mara?'

'Er, no...,' responded Barry, shuffling his feet a little. 'Longleat.'

'Longleat?' queried the Earl.

'Aye. Longleat Safari Park. It's magic, like. And saves yer a load o' hassle from havin' ter fanny aboot gan off somewhere foreign,' Barry explained.

'But...,' began Earl Forsyth.

'Mind you,' continued Barry, not to be put off his stride. 'Last time I went, while I wus drivin' thru the monkey

148

enclosure, some of them little buggers ran off wi' me bloody hubcaps. Thievin' little basta'ds!'

'Surely…,' the Earl attempted to interject again.

'It were worse than drivin' thru Toxteth, if yer kna worra mean!' chuckled Barry.

There was a moment's silence while Barry's comments were fully digested, and then, to everyone's surprise, the Earl actually broke into a grin and began to laugh.

'I say,' he guffawed. 'That's terribly amusing.'

In an instant the whole table were chuckling away, the clergy were trying hard not to snicker, and even Countess Forsyth's dour features managed to crack a smile. Suddenly conversation sprang up from all areas, and, not for the first time, Alice was grateful for the presence of Barry Higgins. The man could spark life into the bleakest of situations.

While the conversation continued to flow, Carstairs busied himself with carrying in a large tureen from the kitchen, which he placed on a nearby table. He began to ladle the contents of the tureen into bowls, which were then placed in front of the guests round the table.

He then stood proudly beside the table and cleared his throat to get the attention of the guests. He announced the starter to be *Brown Windsor Soup*.

Senator Sanderson glanced down, with some trepidation, to examine the bowl of lumpy brown liquid that had been placed in front of him. He hadn't seen anything quite like the contents of the bowl since a fateful business trip to Mexico when the entire delegation had come down with raging dysentery.

He'd heard the British aristocracy were a strange, eccentric bunch, especially when it came to their eating habits. He wanted no part of it.

149

He did notice, however, that all the other diners around the table were spooning the stuff down with relish. He hesitantly took a suspicious sniff and was pleasantly surprised to discover the aroma of beef stock. *Hallelujah*, he thought, *so, it's not a bowl of poop after all*. He managed to finish the soup without any further controversy.

Carstairs has noted the senator's initial reluctance to sample the soup. The butler had prepared the dish from scratch, utilising an ancient family recipe. It'd taken him over an hour to complete. He was pleased when the American had finally taken a taste of the soup and seemed to have enjoyed it.

The soup dishes were cleared and the guests waited patiently with great anticipation for the main course. Senator Sanderson was desperately hoping that he might have at least heard of the next dish due to be served. He had no such luck.

Carstairs took his position at the side of the table again and waited for silence. He announced the main course to be Beef Wellington served with Yorkshire Pudding and seasonal vegetables. The dishes were duly placed down in front of the guests.

Try as he might, Senator Sanderson could see no sign of the promised beef on his plate. Instead, there was a large slab of pastry, and a big brown ball of something unidentifiable. He did at least recognise the vegetables. Slightly perplexed, he raised his hand to attract the attention of the butler and summoned him over. He was sure the Brits were playing tricks on him with their strange humour.

Carstairs dutifully presented himself at the American's side. 'Yes, sir?' he chimed.

'What is…er…this?' asked Earl, indicating the pastry with his knife.

'That is Beef Wellington, sir,' replied the butler.

'You mean there's a *Wellington boot* in there?'

'Most droll, sir,' opined Carstairs acerbically, 'but the name comes from the creator of the dish, Sir Arthur Wellesley...'

Earl was getting more and more confused, and as a consequence, was starting to get irritated.

'Arthur Wellesley? Who the hell is he? Some kind of half-assed, wimpy, cook?'

'He was the Duke of Wellington, sir. The Iron Duke. One of the finest generals the world has ever known.'

'Oh...okay,' said Earl, relenting a little. 'So, what did he do with the beef?'

'The beef is inside the pastry, sir.'

The scales fell from Earl's eyes as he cut into the pastry and discovered the fillet steak inside, cooked to perfection.

'Well,' declared the senator, 'that's one way to ruin a good steak!'

'If you say so, sir.'

'Okay,' continued Earl, who now believed he was getting to the bottom of this culinary mystery. 'And what is this brown ball for?'

'That is a Yorkshire Pudding, sir,' Carstairs informed him. 'You eat it.'

'For dessert?'

'Dessert, sir?'

'You said it's a pudding, didn't you?'

'Ah, I see your point, sir,' admitted Carstairs.

'Oh, good,' said Earl. 'Then perhaps you could enlighten me, as I'm finding the whole meal experience to be more of a cryptic mind teaser!'

Carstairs was kicking himself. He'd been intent on impressing the Americans with traditional British dishes, but it hadn't occurred to him that they'd find it confusing and off-putting.

'It was originally a dessert, sir, you are quite correct,' the butler concurred. 'But for the last few hundred years it has also been eaten as an accompaniment to a main course. It is made of batter, sir, and is quite delicious.'

Satisfied, Earl finally began to eat the main course. He tried a mouthful of the Beef Wellington.

'Hey, Carstairs,' he proclaimed over a mouthful of steak and pastry, 'It ain't half bad!'

Carstairs was relieved to hear him say so. 'Thank you, sir.' He smiled graciously at the senator.

'It could just do with a bit of a pep up, though,' said Earl. 'Say, you got any mustard back there in the kitchen?'

'Certainly, sir, I'll fetch you some.'

Carstairs drifted off to the kitchen and returned moments later with a pot of finest English mustard. He placed it down on the table next to Earl.

'Thank you,' said the senator politely, and began spooning the mustard liberally onto the side of his plate. He cut off another piece of the Beef Wellington and daubed it in the mustard, giving it a generous coating.

'If I may advocate caution, sir,' advised the butler, 'English mustard is significantly stronger than…'

'Thank you, Carstairs,' interrupted Earl. 'I don't need any more history lessons, thank you.'

152

'As you wish, sir.'

The senator smiled smugly at the butler and then stuffed the entire forkful of food into his mouth. He took a few thoughtful chews. And then he experienced a sensation as if a volcano were erupting in his mouth. It felt as though red-hot flames were shooting through his brain and out of his nose. His eyes were streaming tears and his face was turning a worrying shade of purple.

'Holy shit!' he managed to splutter. 'My mouth's on goddamn fire!'

The assembled clergy gave him a disapproving look.

He looked frantically around his place setting searching for something to quench the heat. Carstairs came to his rescue by placing a large glass of water beside the stricken American. He'd anticipated that this might be the senator's reaction. Earl grabbed the glass and downed it in one. He gasped for breath as he tried to recover.

'I did attempt to warn you, sir,' stated Carstairs in a supercilious manner.

Franco had thoroughly enjoyed the exhibition and was hooting with laughter at his employer's misfortune. The senator gave him a murderous look. The other guests were looking on with concern.

'Are you all right, Senator?' asked Alice anxiously. The evening wasn't going quite as well as she'd hoped.

'I'll be fine in a moment,' he responded, slowly returning to a more natural colour.

'Hey, boss, better take it a little easier on the mustard, huh?' Franco teased him.

'One more wisecrack out of you, *Clunk*, and you'll be joining the limo at the bottom of the moat, y'hear!' warned the senator with a furious scowl.

153

Franco pretended to look chastened.

*

Everyone resumed tucking into their main course and a relative normality returned to the proceedings. Humphrey decided to start the ball rolling with regard to the situation at Sunderland docks. He asked the senator what his intentions were likely to be with dealing with the strike action.

'I'm glad you asked,' replied Earl seriously, 'as I have devised a plan on how I intend to deal with those layabouts. But I need your assurance that everyone around this table is totally trustworthy and that what I have to say will remain completely secret and confidential. Loose lips will sink my ships, you understand?'

'I can personally vouch for each and every person gathered here tonight. You have my word. What is said in this room will stay in this room,' Humphrey stated solemnly.

'That's good to know,' stated Earl, 'because I'm going to need some help.'

'You may rest assured that everyone around this table is one hundred percent behind you, Senator,' Humphrey confirmed. 'And my daughter will do anything in her power to assist you, I'm sure.'

'Absolutely,' agreed Alice. 'But in what way can we help you, Senator?'

'Well, I intend to inform the union and the dock workers that unless work resumes in Sunderland docks forthwith, then I will have no alternative but to recruit a new workforce, and the previous workers will subsequently lose their jobs.'

There were gasps of shock from around the table at the audacious plan.

'I'm not sure you'd get away with that,' Alice advised.

'Now hold your horses and hear me out,' continued the senator. 'It's only a bluff. I'm just going to pretend to hire new workers, you get me? I just need to make it look as though the dockyard is operating again. And without the union's say so – and without the current striking workforce. You get it? And this is what I need your help for.'

'Okay,' said Alice. 'I'm starting to get the picture. Can you be more specific what you need from us?'

'Absolutely,' confirmed Earl. 'For instance, I'm sure we'll need licences and consents from the local government to operate the machinery again. I was hoping that would be something you could arrange for me, Ms Chesham? Perhaps with your father's assistance too?'

Alice looked down the table to where Humphrey was sitting and gave him a questioning glance.

'Pater?' she asked. 'Do you think we could do that?'

'I'm quite sure we could manage it,' Humphrey replied, 'if we all put our heads together.' He gave a knowing nod to Carstairs, who acknowledged the subtle request for his services with a slight bow.

'Excellent,' declared the senator. 'And Mr Higgins?'

Barry sat up in his seat at the mention of his name and turned his attention to Earl.

'Aye, Senator,' he responded. 'What can I dee fer ye?'

'You used to work on the docks, right?'

'Aye, I did.'

155

'So, you can operate the gantry cranes and other machinery?'

'I can, aye.'

'You think you could help out with supervising the machines? And maybe run one of the cranes so it looks like they're all working?'

'Nay wurries,' confirmed Barry. 'Piece o' cake, like.'

'That's great, buddy.' Earl smiled at him gratefully. 'And Reggie? I sure could use your help too.'

Reggie was gobsmacked that the senator was asking for his help. But given the generosity that Earl had shown towards getting the Dockers club refurbished, and giving Reggie the opportunity to manage the place, he was absolutely ready to do his best to help out. He reached for Alice's hand under the table, and as he held it, she gave him a reassuring squeeze.

'Do you think you could find, say, a dozen guys to come and put on some high viz jackets and pretend to be working the docks? I'd pay them handsomely for their time, of course.'

Reggie could think of about a hundred guys that'd be willing to do it. A lot of folks were looking for any kind of work right now. Times were hard. He could only guess what the senator's idea of being paid handsomely was, but he was sure it would be in excess of most people's wildest dreams.

'No problem,' Reggie stated simply.

Earl grinned happily. It seemed his plan was working out just fine. He turned his attention back to Alice. He noted she was looking apprehensive.

'And, Ms Chesham, I have not forgotten about plan B,' he assured her. 'Your idea to take on Mr Finch at his own game is an excellent idea and I absolutely want you to

156

continue your scheme of implementing environmentally sound innovations to the business. And rest assured, if my little plan doesn't work out, then we will be running full steam ahead with your proposals. Okay?'

'Okay,' agreed Alice. 'Fair enough.' She gave him her best winning smile, and he grinned back.

Humphrey was pleased that they'd managed to discuss the senator's plans and were able to help him. At least this part of the evening had gone well.

*

The main course plates had been cleared away ten minutes ago. Carstairs had allowed for a propitious amount of time to elapse, so that the business talk that was taking place could be concluded satisfactorily. He had listened in on the senator's plans with great interest. But the business talk had now concluded, and Carstairs decided it was time to serve the dessert.

He took up his station at the side of the dining table once again and gave a gentle cough to cease the hubbub of conversation. He took great pleasure in announcing the dessert to be Spotted Dick with Custard. There ensued some excited oohs and aahs from the ecstatic group of clergymen.

Senator Sanderson, on the other hand, was sincerely hoping against hope that he had misheard the butler. But when his dessert dish was placed in front of him, and he took a cursory peek, he discovered to his horror that he had heard him perfectly correctly.

As Earl stared down at his gruesome dessert, there appeared to be, at best guess, the large phallus of an unknown animal, lying in the bowl, staring back at him. As if that wasn't bad enough, it did indeed appear to be infected with some unsightly venereal disease as it was completely covered in spots. To make matters even worse, some sort of yellow pus had discharged into the bowl next to it. He started to feel nauseous and bile rose to the back of his throat.

Earl glanced over at Franco, who was also staring, aghast, down into his dessert bowl. Earl knew Franco would eat almost anything but even he was baulking at this one. *What the hell are these crazy limeys serving us now?* he wondered with dread. There was nothing else for it and he had to raise his hand to summon the butler once again. Carstairs duly sauntered over to the senator's side.

'Yes, sir?' Carstairs enquired calmly.

'Do you think,' requested Earl, with just a hint of tetchiness, 'that I might have a dessert that doesn't consist of a Johnson with an STD?'

'I'm not sure I get your meaning, sir,' remarked Carstairs in confusion.

'I mean…that!' said Earl, pointing at his dessert dish. He then raised his eyebrows enquiringly at the butler.

'But, sir, *that* is merely a sponge roly-poly.'

Unconvinced, the senator examined the dessert in more detail. 'And these spots?' he demanded to know.

'Currants, sir.'

'And what about all this pus?' asked Earl, carefully extracting a small sample with his spoon and thrusting it under the butler's nose.

'It's crème Anglais, sir. Otherwise known as custard.'

'I see,' said Earl, feeling slightly foolish.

'Will that be all, sir?'

158

'Why, yes, thank you, Carstairs,' replied the senator bashfully. 'Well done.'

'A pleasure, sir.'

Earl and Franco hastily began to eat their desserts so as not to cause further offence. Baroness Harriet Billingbrooke, having overheard the exchange, was staring over at the senator with a bemused smirk on her lips. She had to admit the senator was decidedly entertaining and resolved to get to know him better.

Once dessert was finished, Humphrey and Henrietta invited their guests through to their magnificent opulent drawing room for coffee and brandy. Earl, eager to leave the table before anything else dubious was presented to him, followed the hosts quickly through to the drawing room. He settled himself on one of the Chesterfield sofas near the vast, oak beamed, inglenook fireplace. Before Franco had a chance to join his boss, Baroness Billingbrooke had flown gracefully across the room and plumped herself down next to Earl, much to his surprise.

Before the senator knew it, Harriet had hooked her arm around his and was gazing up into his face as though trying to read his mind. Earl was a little unsettled by her forthright approach. No woman had ever manhandled him like this. He sat next to her awkwardly, but his pulse rate was rising rapidly.

'Now, then,' she cooed, 'we didn't get off to the best start, did we?'

'No, ma'am,' replied Earl. Somehow, she was making him feel like a naughty schoolboy.

'Well…why don't we just forget about the little incident earlier on, and start again?' she suggested, as if writing off his $250,000 limousine was a minor botheration.

'Sure, we can do that,' Earl replied magnanimously.

'Good-oh!' she smiled at him. 'I knew you'd be a sport.'

Earl smiled back. 'It's just a car,' he shrugged.

She nodded in agreement. She was starting to take a shine to the senator. She even found him quite charming in a rugged, unsophisticated way.

Their conversation paused momentarily while Carstairs passed by, serving coffees and brandies.

Once he'd moved on Harriet suddenly grasped Earl's arm harder, looked at him conspiratorially, and glanced left and right before she spoke.

'Do you like to shoot, Senator?' she asked secretively.

'Ma'am, I'm from Texas,' he answered. 'I was practically born with a gun in my hand. My trademark as a Southern politician is to shoot my Colt 45 in the air, especially when I'm on a winning streak!'

'Well, that would explain your impression of Yosemite Sam upon your arrival!' she ribbed him, with a grin.

Even when she was insulting him, he was still captivated by her.

'I get carried away, at times,' he admitted, grinning back. 'Please call me Earl, by the way.'

'Okay, Earl...and you can call me...Baroness Billingbrooke.'

Earl looked crestfallen. 'Huh?'

She laughed and wrinkled her nose at him. 'I'm just kidding, Earl. You are going to be such fun to tease! You can call me Harri.'

Earl looked relieved. 'Nice to meet you, Harri.'

'So, what do you say to some clay pigeon shooting tomorrow morning? You think you can beat me?' she challenged him.

'I ain't never shot no clay pigeons before, Harri. But I can shoot with the best of 'em, don't you worry about that.'

'Well, it's a date then,' she said tantalisingly. 'Bring your friend with you if he'd like to come. Shall we say 10am?'

'We'll be there!' he replied happily.

'And after lunch, Alice wants to take us out on the horses. Do you ride well too, cowboy?'

'You betcha!'

Harriet leaned over even closer to the senator.

'I see I shall have to watch you *very* closely!' she breathed in his ear.

And with that, she stood up from the sofa, downed her brandy in one, and bade Earl and the room goodnight. She sauntered out of the drawing room and headed upstairs, leaving the senator looking as pleased as the cat who got the cream.

Franco, having watched the two of them canoodling on the sofa, came over to his boss and gave him his considered opinion.

'That dame is nuts,' he said to the senator frankly.

'Yeah, I know,' murmured Earl, 'but there's something about her I can't help but like…'

Franco looked at his employer with pity. 'Not me, boss,' he stated firmly. 'I've only known her for a few hours and she's already run me off the road, attacked me with an umbrella, and sent me to the back of the line like I'm some goddamn little punk.'

'Yeah. Isn't she amazing!' enthused Earl dreamily.

Franco shook his head in disbelief. Soon after, the party began to break up as the various dignitaries and acquaintances bade their goodnights and made their way out to the driveway to find their cars to head back home. The remaining guests, who were staying for the night, slowly made their way up the grand galleried staircase to the landing, where Carstairs directed them down various corridors to their respective bedrooms.

After a tumultuous evening, Humphrey and Henrietta turned in thinking that although things hadn't gone quite to plan, they had at least firmly aligned the Cheshams to Senator Sanderson's cause. And that could only be a good thing, especially for Alice. Henrietta was also pleased to see that her sister was behaving more agreeably towards their American guests.

*

A hearty full English breakfast was served the following morning. Barry, in particular, enjoyed the repast, having had his plate topped up at least three times by the attentive Carstairs. Barry was having a whale of a time as a guest at Chesham Manor. He'd never experienced anything like it in his life. Alice had promised to take him on a morning walk afterwards, through the formal grounds and gardens. Henrietta and Humphrey had expressed a wish to join them.

Alfie was desperate to show Reggie the electric guitar and amp that he had set up in one of the spare rooms upstairs. Alice could tell that Reggie was just as keen as Alfie to check out the music system. And so, with her blessing, Reggie and Alfie had disappeared upstairs where presently a cacophony of electric screeches sounded out as Alfie attempted to impress Reggie with some mangled power chords. It would appear Reggie was going to have his work cut out for him in trying to make Alfie into a budding musical prodigy.

The remaining party, consisting of Baroness Billingbrooke, Senator Sanderson, Franco and Carstairs, were piling into a topline Range Rover parked at the back of the manor. In a trailer, attached to the towing bar of the vehicle, was a clay pigeon throwing trap, several boxes of clays, some ammunition, and three beautifully made Purdey double-barrelled shotguns.

Carstairs drove the Range Rover off down the driveway and then veered off down a farm track heading to a large field some distance away from the house. The Baroness was sat in the front seat next to the butler, while the Americans were sprawled out in the back. Presently the Range Rover bumped to a stop next to a large circular mown section of grass at the near end of the field. Carstairs took a moment to position the vehicle so that the trailer containing the clay pigeon throwing trap was pointing out across the field. He then applied the handbrake and turned off the engine. On exiting the driver's side, he donned a light brown workman's style overall to protect his butler's uniform. He also pulled a plain cloth flat cap onto his head.

The Baroness was attired more formally in a smart tweed suit consisting of plus-fours, waistcoat and jacket. She also wore a tweed flat cap to shield the sunlight from her eyes. The suit fitted her body snugly, and the senator could not help but admire her figure. She certainly kept herself in shape. His heartbeat was aflutter once again.

Earl was dressed less formally in a cowboy style. He wore jeans, leather boots and a Western style shirt. He trademark Stetson was perched firmly on his head. Franco, as was his norm, was dressed in his habitual, neatly cut, black suit.

Carstairs rummaged in the back of the trailer and emerged holding the three Purdeys. He passed the shotguns out to the shooting party. Earl examined the gun carefully. He could see that the quality of the firearm was exceptional. The weighting and balance was perfect. It was exquisitely engraved with scenes of a hunting nature. It was a fine shotgun. Franco, too, was equally impressed.

The Baroness had opened the break-action of her own Purdey, and had the shotgun hooked casually over one arm. She was standing, slouched against the Range Rover, effortlessly exuding confidence and style.

'Are we ready then, chaps?' she teased Earl and Franco with a bemused smile.

Earl was impressed, yet again, with her assertiveness and élan and couldn't believe she was actually egging them on.

As it happened, Harriet had every reason to come across confidently with the gun. She was one of the finest shots in the county and had a trophy cabinet at home positively stuffed full of silverware. She gave Carstairs a nod to load up the clay pigeon trap and make it ready. She then took two shotgun cartridges from the ammunition box and loaded both barrels of her Purdey. Knowing she had the full attention of Earl and Franco, she flashed them a cheeky smile and walked up to the edge of the shooting circle. She closed the Purdey's action, cocked the hammers and readied the gun in her shoulder. She then removed the safety catch.

'Pull!' she exclaimed loudly to Carstairs, who dutifully worked the mechanism of the trap. Two clays were flung from the machine, high into the air and fifty yards across the field. There were two rapid pops from Harriet's shotgun and both clays instantly disappeared in a cloud of debris. The Americans looked on, impressed with her skill.

To assert this was no fluke, she reloaded the Purdey with two more cartridges, took up her position once more and yelled 'Pull!' again. Two more clays flew out across the field and were dispatched as quickly and cleanly as the first time. Harriet broke the action of her shotgun, removed the spent cartridges and sauntered over to where Earl and Franco were stood gawping at her.

'Your turn, boys,' she stated sweetly as she blew them a sassy kiss.

Senator Earl Sanderson III was falling in love. Not only was this woman bold, authoritative and confident, but she could handle a firearm far better than almost anyone he'd ever met. To Earl, she was the most evocative, tantalising and attractive woman in the world. He couldn't get over that she wasn't in the slightest bit intimidated by him. Far from it, in fact. She seemed to positively thrive on matching his bravado and clearly relished teasing and goading him. And he *loved* it.

Moving as if he were floating on air, Earl walked trancelike over to the shooting circle, selected two cartridges and loaded his shotgun. He lifted it to his shoulder.

'Pull!' he drawled languidly.

Carstairs operated the machine and two clays were flown out over the field. Earl's shotgun sounded twice. One clay disintegrated into bits, but the other fell unscathed into the meadow.

'Darn it,' he cursed, shaking his head ruefully. *He never missed.*

'Butterfingers!' Harriet scolded him. She was delighted he'd fudged it.

The senator quickly reloaded the Purdey. He squinted his eyes in concentration and physically pulled himself together.

'Pull!' he commanded firmly.

This time there was no mistake. Both shots met their targets and the clays were blown to bits.

'Good show!' cheered the Baroness gleefully. 'Not bad...for a Yankee.'

Earl smiled graciously and doffed his Stetson at her as he made his way back.

Next up was Franco. In a meticulously professional manner, which was truly awe-inspiring, he strode up to the shooting circle and had loaded the shotgun and readied it at his shoulder in the blink of an eye.

'Pull!' he shouted ominously.

The two clays were barely out of the machine when two blasts sounded and they were gone.

In a heartbeat the gun was reloaded and readied again.

'Pull!' he yelled again.

Two more clays exploded with deadly efficiency. Franco lowered the weapon, allowed himself a grimace of satisfaction, and moved to rejoin the group.

'Bloody hell! He's a bit useful, isn't he?' said Harriet, elbowing Earl in the ribs. 'He should shoot professionally, I reckon.'

'Well, he does. Kinda,' acknowledged Earl.

Harriet looked at him quizzically and then shrugged.

'Fancy another round?' she asked happily.

'You betcha!' he replied. *Damn, he loved this dame!*

*

166

A light lunch, once again prepared by the ever-reliable Carstairs, had been served to the guests. Earl was relieved to see that the luncheon simply comprised a variety of sandwiches and salads. Now *that* he could get a grip on. Although he did come across a sandwich that appeared to consist entirely of cucumber, which he did find a little bit bizarre.

Alice caught up with her brother, Alfie, over lunch and the two of them had discussed how they were each getting on in their new roles. Including the subsequent disasters they'd each suffered. They'd noted, with resignation, the irony of the situation that Alfie (being a disreputable lush) would not have been half as affected as Alice was with the drinks spiking incident, while Alice would certainly not have fallen for the fake Tracy Island story which had been Alfie's undoing. If only they'd been able to trade places in those scenarios!

After the meal had concluded and the guests were replete, everyone split up into several smaller groups to pass the afternoon.

Alfie and Reggie resumed their guitar session. Reggie had succeeded in teaching Alfie how to play three or four chords cleanly, and he was sounding a whole lot better. Reggie was hoping he'd be able to teach him to do all the major chords properly before the day was through. The two men were becoming firm friends.

Humphrey and Carstairs had retired to Humphrey's study to discuss making a start on acquiring the permits Earl had requested for the dockyard. It was going to take some wrangling with the council. Of that, there was no doubt, but Humphrey had great faith in Carstairs' ability to procure the necessary documents.

Barry had joined Franco in trying to salvage what items they were able to from the wreck of the stretch limo.

167

They had utilised the ladder again as a makeshift gangplank to reach the car from the bankside of the moat. The sunroof was still open and Franco was lowering Barry down through it into the interior of the car. The inside was still quite dry. Only an inch or two of water had managed to seep in so far. At Barry's suggestion, the salvage operation had begun with rescuing the contents of the onboard bar.

The remaining group was gathering by the stables, which were located inside a huge, ancient oak beamed barn. The barn was one of the oldest buildings on the estate. Alice had invited all those able and willing to ride to join her on a trek around the grounds. The equestrian group consisted of herself, her mother, Aunt Harri and Earl. She was thrilled too, to see her beloved horse Jonty again. She'd missed him terribly. They mounted up and headed off across the estate towards the Polo Club, on the same route Alice had taken about a month ago, when she'd made her last rally as the MP for North Norfolk.

Harriet had changed her outfit to one more suitable for riding. Akin to Alice and Henrietta, she now wore jodhpurs, leather riding boots, a black riding jacket and helmet. Senator Sanderson was riding behind her and was certainly appreciating the view of her derrière bouncing up and down in front of him as she rode along. A lustful pang, which he hadn't experienced in a long time, began to form deep within him.

His gaze had not gone unnoticed by Harriet as she had turned her head to observe how well he rode and had caught him ogling at her bottom. Not that she minded overly. She was rather enjoying the attention he was so brazenly giving her.

If truth were known, Harriet had quite the racy libido herself. Her late husband, Baron Eric Billingbrooke, had done his best to satisfy her desires in that department, but being some twenty years older than his wife, he had not even come close to the mark, and had eventually given up on the job altogether. Over the last five years, Harriet's attention had subsequently wandered to more virile and varied partners to satisfy her carnal cravings. She was not averse to the sapphic pleasures either. Her sexual orientation had always been a bit of a mixed bag. Since she was a teenager, she'd discovered she found both men and women equally attractive. And these days it was well known among her household staff, and in the local village, that she was quite happy to swing both ways. And so, it had all been rather unfortunate, when one day last summer, the Baron had come home early from his habitual afternoon stroll and had walked into the bedroom to find Harriet sandwiched between the stableboy and the housemaid writhing around in the act of a raunchy threesome. The shock had been too much for the old boy's dicky ticker and he'd keeled over onto the chaise longue and promptly kicked the bucket. It'd taken the undertaker hours to get the look off his face. Harriet had been the sole heir to the Billingbrooke Estate and was now, in her own right, one of the wealthiest landowners in the county. She could certainly give Humphrey and Henrietta a run for their money.

The equestrian group had reached the Polo Club and stopped for a brief rest. They'd shared a jug of fresh lemonade on the club's terrace before mounting up again and heading back to Chesham Manor. Alice and Henrietta were the first to arrive back at the stables and they entered the vast wooden barn to begin to untack their horses. Alice had just removed Jonty's saddle when Harriet and Earl rode back into the compound. Harriet dismounted and led her horse into the stable to join Henrietta and Alice. A stable hand took Earl's horse away for him, leaving him standing alone in the courtyard. Curiosity soon got the better of him and he wondered where the ladies had got to. He decided to follow them into the barn.

The stable was dark and cool inside. The wooden double doors to the barn were ajar and flooded the interior with sunlight. Earl spotted Harriet about halfway down the stable block and began to walk over to join her. Behind him,

Alice and Henrietta had finished untacking their horses and were heading back outside. As Earl reached the stable where Harriet was, he saw she had just untacked her own horse. She had her back to him and didn't hear him as he approached. As he came up behind her she bent over to release the buckle of her riding boot. Her prim behind was thrust out towards him and the yearning in his loins was almost too strong for him to bear. Alice and Henrietta had just walked out of the stable block and the large wooden entrance doors swung closed behind them, plunging the stables into near darkness. Earl bumped gently into Harriet and as he felt her stand back up, he slid his arms around her waist and held her to him. She turned in his arms to face him and he moved his head closer to hers with the intention of kissing her passionately.

Harriet had just undone the buckle on her riding boot when the whole stable block suddenly fell into blackness. At the same instant she sensed movement behind her and she stood up abruptly. Strong arms entwined roughly around her waist and, terrified, she twisted round to face her assailant and, struggling desperately, she prepared to defend herself.

Earl felt Harriet stirring in his arms, exciting his desire for her even more. He puckered up his mouth to plant a fervent kiss on her lips.

Instead, and much to his surprise, a delicate hand, bunched into a tight fist, came flying out of the darkness and socked him solidly in his left eye. Seeing stars, he howled in pain, and then a neatly jodhpurred knee connected soundly with his nether regions. He fell to the floor in agony and formed a foetal position, cupping his hands over his groin.

The large stable doors were flung open again as Alice and Henrietta re-entered the building looking for Earl and Harriet. As light flooded in, they stopped in their tracks as they saw the sorry spectacle before them. Senator Sanderson was lying hunched up on the stable floor groaning softly to himself. Baroness Billingbrooke, realising with shock and horror that her fierce assailant was in fact her most ardent admirer, was beside herself with remorse. She threw herself down on her knees beside Earl, removed his Stetson hat, and cradled his head in her lap. She peppered his forehead with apologetic kisses.

'I'm so, so, sorry,' she lamented. 'If only I'd known it was you…but I thought you were outside…and I thought I was being attacked, you see…and…oh, dear…I do hope there's no hard feelings.'

'Not any more there ain't,' groaned Earl, still nursing his now inert genitalia.

'I really don't know what to say by way of an apology,' Harriet cried ruefully, 'but perhaps this may help…'

She leant over and kissed the senator tenderly and meaningfully on his lips. Earl's eyes blinked rapidly with bewilderment, and then, slowly but surely, a contented smile reappeared on his face. As she helped him to his feet, she placed his arm over her shoulders and together they made their way back to the main house.

'Ma'am,' Earl said to her sincerely, 'you are one hell of a piece of work, you know that?'

'It's been mentioned, yes,' concurred Harriet.

'But I do believe I'm falling for you,' he said earnestly.

'That's so sweet,' she replied warmly, and she knew in her heart that the feeling was mutual.

*

An hour or so later, it was time for the guests to depart. They began to congregate in the manor's entrance hall to say their goodbyes before departing. As the Americans'

171

vehicle was somewhat indisposed, Humphrey had offered the use of the Range Rover to get them all back to Sunderland. Alice would have to drive as she was the only one insured for it, but she had no problem with that. Carstairs would travel up on the train in a few days' time to bring it back again.

The senator was just thanking Humphrey and Henrietta for their hospitality and assistance when Barry and Franco reappeared from their salvage operation. As Franco entered the hall, he took a quick glance at his employer and frowned in consternation. He'd noted the injury to the senator's eye. It was starting to swell up quite spectacularly.

'Hey, boss! What gives?' he questioned Earl with concern. 'I leave you for a few hours and you get yourself roughed up!'

'I had an accident while riding,' the senator stated, giving Harriet a cursory nod.

'Oh, right,' said Franco, accepting the story without argument. 'Yeah, those horses sure can be flighty.'

Harriet sidled up to where Earl was standing and embraced him warmly, kissing him respectfully on both cheeks.

'That was kind of you,' she whispered softly in his ear. 'And I'll repay the favour very soon.' She gave him a saucy wink, unobserved by the others.

'Ma'am,' replied Earl with a grin, doffing his Stetson at her for good measure.

'And this is my card,' she announced formally, handing him her address and number. 'I'd be obliged for a call to inform me when you arrive back safely.'

Harriet did like to keep things above board, but she wasn't really kidding anyone. Everyone had observed the obvious relationship that was developing between her and the

172

senator. Alice had certainly never seen her aunt hand out her card to anyone before. She hoped it was a good thing.

Alfie and Reggie materialised on the landing and made their way down the grand staircase to join the group. Once everyone had said their goodbyes, they made their way into the courtyard where the vehicles were parked.

Harriet opened the driver's door to her yellow Lotus sports car and slipped behind the wheel. Her pussycat, Galore, was in her travel crate on the passenger seat. The car shot off like a bullet, wheel-spinning across the drawbridge, and whizzed off down the long drive at dizzying speed. Baroness Billingbrooke's estate was located roughly an hour away, further along the North Norfolk coast towards Cromer. It was a lovely scenic drive back along the coast road, passing through many gorgeous and impeccably presented seaside villages along the way.

The rest of the group piled into the Range Rover and made a more sedate departure back across the drawbridge and up the sweeping drive. Franco, being the biggest, was in the front passenger seat, while Earl, Reggie and Barry were in the back. Reggie was in the middle, being the smallest. Alice turned the Range Rover out onto the main road and headed towards King's Lynn. From there, they took the A17 to Newark-on-Trent, and then the A1 back up north towards Sunderland.

14.

Franco was in the driver's seat of Earl III, the final limousine in the senator's cavalcade. He was driving the car out of its container and onto the quayside next to the Lone Star freighter, the MS Yellow Rose. Earl Sanderson, whose left eye was heavily bruised and swollen after the pummelling he'd received from Baroness Billingbrooke, was standing on the gangway. He began bawling advice at his bodyguard on how to successfully perform the operation.

After enduring ten minutes of the senator's pointless hollering, Franco had the limo released from its housing, unscathed, and safely parked up on the dockside.

Moments later a Mini Countryman came whizzing through the docklands, turned along the quayside and parked up next to the limo. In a state of high excitement, Alice, Barry and Reggie alighted from the vehicle and hurried up to the Americans. Alice was waving a handful of documents at them and smiling broadly.

'We did it!' she exclaimed triumphantly. 'We got the permits!'

The senator beamed at her with appreciation.

'Can we do it!' he yelled happily. 'Hell, yeah!'

He reached into his jacket and pulled the imitation gun from its holster. He fired several shots into the air in celebration, causing everyone in the vicinity to jump out of their skins. They were relieved when he holstered the gun again.

'So, it's all set for Friday,' enthused Alice. 'I'm sure the dockers will confirm they'll be attending. Along with the union boss and Alan Bailey. It's great news!'

'Sure is,' Earl agreed. 'I don't know how you arranged the paperwork so fast, but I sure am grateful to you.'

'Well, to be honest, Carstairs was the main player in that department,' confessed Alice. 'But Pater and I exerted as much influence as we could to speed the process along.'

'I'm sure glad to have you all on my team,' said Earl with great sincerity. 'Say, now we have the permits, why don't we have a little test run of the equipment? Could you do that for me, Mr Higgins?'

'Nay problem,' Barry assured him. 'You jus' tell me what ye want deein, an I'll dee it.'

Earl took a moment to gaze at all the machinery currently lying idle on the dockside. Presently, he made up his mind what he wanted Barry to do.

'Okay, pal. So, I think it would be good if we have some of these gantry cranes looking like they're working on offloading some of the cargo from my freighter. And then…I dunno…anything else you can think of, I guess.'

Barry nodded in understanding, and, feeling full of importance, he happily climbed into the cabin of the first gantry crane and started it up. He positioned the hoisting arm over the cargo area of the MS Yellow Rose to look as if it were in the process of unloading. He then climbed down from the cabin and went over to the second gantry crane. Climbing into the second cabin he started it up but this time he engaged the lifting magnet. He skilfully manoeuvred the magnet over the top of the container that had contained the third limousine and placed the magnet down plumb in the centre. Turning the magnet on, he lifted the huge container high up over the dockside and left it dangling as if it were in the process of being moved. Lastly Barry went over to where the forklifts

175

were stored and drove two of them out onto the dockside to make it look as if they were in use to move any unloaded cargo. Once he'd finished, he returned to where the group were still standing.

'How's that then?' he asked Earl. 'Lookin' aboot reet?'

'Perfect!' Earl smiled happily. 'Nice job, Barry!'

'Nay wurries,' replied Barry with a grin.

The senator then turned his attention to Reggie. 'Mr Hill?' he enquired,' do you have your friends ready to play their roles?'

'I got a dozen lads coming to help out,' replied Reggie. 'Don't worry. They won't let you down.'

Earl had given Reggie two thousand four hundred pounds to pay them for their time. When Reggie had offered them two hundred pounds each for a few hours of their time, he'd nearly had his hand bitten off.

'Great news, Reggie,' said Earl. 'You have my thanks.'

'We're all ready for Friday, then?' asked Alice.

'We sure are, ma'am!'

The senator looked mighty pleased with himself. He had every confidence in his plan and was sure that the docks would be back running smoothly very soon.

*

Len Finch was sat at his desk in his office located in the trade union building in central Sunderland. He was stroking his chin and musing over the fact that he'd heard very little from the opposition in the last week or so. He'd thought it odd the senator had not made his next move yet. He knew the Tory woman, Chesham, was toadying up to him in a blatant attempt to improve her own fortunes. No surprise there. But he did wonder what the pair of them were up to. His thoughts were interrupted by a knocking on his office door.

'Enter!' he commanded self-importantly.

The languid features of Derek Barlow appeared around the door as he slithered into the room. He was clutching a letter in his hand that he now presented to his new employer.

'This was received, recorded delivery, by the office first thing this morning,' he reported officiously.

'Oh,' replied Len with interest. 'What is it?'

'It's a formal notice from Lone Star Freight requesting the presence of the trade union and the dock workers down by the quayside on Friday morning. A carbon copy has been issued to both the Labour and Conservative parties also.'

'What on earth is the notice for?' queried Len.

'It says the Chairman, Senator Sanderson III, wishes to address all concerned in a very important announcement,' replied Derek.

'Foghorn Leghorn wants to address us, does he?' sneered Len. 'That should be interesting. Does it say what about exactly?'

'It just says it's regarding the future of Sunderland docks and its workforce,' responded Derek.

Len Finch did not like the sound of that. It sounded to him very much like a thinly veiled threat. But he wasn't going to be intimidated by some capitalist dog. He'd show them who was in charge.

'Please reply to them, brother, and tell them we accept the invitation,' said Len.

'Yes, comrade,' chanted Derek in reply.

'And when you've done that,' continued Len, 'I'll need you to make up a dozen placards for the workers to carry with them. They are to state: Strike Action! Workers Unite! Down with Capitalism! Respect Our Rights! Fair Pay For Fair Work! That sort of thing. You get the idea?'

'Yes, comrade.'

'And as your valiant leader I will march alongside my brothers and sisters and together we will face our nemesis. We are all equal in our common endeavour, are we not, brother?'

'Yes, comrade,' stated Derek loyally.

But what Mr Barlow didn't know, was that Mr Finch fervently believed that some were more equal than others. Which, of course, was the stuff of Orwellian nightmares.

*

The event had been scheduled to start at 10am on Friday. Earl had requested that his team all show up an hour earlier so they had time to set the scene. At 9am sharp, Alice drove into the docks in her Mini Countryman and parked up near the MS Yellow Rose. Shortly afterwards, a battered minibus driven by Reggie pulled up next to her, and about ten scruffy looking lads alighted and stood around looking nervous. Finally, Barry drew up alongside in his Austin Montego. He'd given a lift to another two lads who hadn't

178

been able to fit in the minibus. Barry went round to the back of his car and opened the boot. He lifted out a dozen high-viz jackets and work helmets. Reggie took them off him and passed them around to his colleagues. Once they'd put them on, the scene looked considerably more professional.

'Good morning, y'all!' came a booming Texan accent from the top of the gangway of the MS Yellow Rose. 'Let's get this show on the road!'

Senator Earl Sanderson III bowled down the gangway festooned in his finest Western suit, complete with Stetson and jingling cowboy boots. Although he was still sporting a vivid looking black eye, he still looked impressively smart and domineering. Behind him loomed the towering black suited frame of his bodyguard, Franco Gambini.

On hearing the booming authoritative voice, the recruited lads all turned to stare in awe at the larger-than-life Americans.

'Okay!' bawled Earl getting himself fired up. 'Now you listen up! Mr Higgins here is your supervisor for today. Y'all listen to him and do *exactly* what he tells you. Y'hear?'

There was a smattering of acknowledgements from the lads.

'All right, then!' continued Earl. 'Barry, let's get these boys busy!'

'Aye-aye, boss!' responded Barry and snapped into action.

He first placed two of the group in the forklifts that he'd driven into place several days ago. He started the engines for them and just told them to hold the wheel and look like they were driving. Nothing more. He then placed another lad in the cabin of the first gantry crane that was positioned over the hold of the freighter. Again, Barry switched the machine

179

on and gave strict instructions to just sit there and touch nothing. Another eight lads he positioned at random around the docks and just told them to walk about looking busy. As an extra touch, he gave some of them some clipboards to hold so that it looked like they were working through an inventory.

That left one lad remaining. A spotty uninspiring youth with a runny nose. He was named Kevin. He was positioned in the second gantry crane that was holding the container aloft with the magnet. Kevin was looking at all the controls in the cabin with great consternation.

'Don't fret, lad. You're not to do owt, okay.' Barry instructed him firmly. 'Just divvun't touch anything, and you'll be reet. Okay, son?'

'Areet,' murmured Kevin, looking petrified.

Barry gave him a friendly pat on the shoulder, climbed down from the cabin, and then returned to where Earl was standing. The senator was watching the proceedings with great pleasure. The docks looked alive with activity.

'How's that lookin'? asked Barry.

'Looking good, Mr Higgins. It's looking good!' replied Earl.

Barry flashed a wink over to where Alice and Reggie were standing by the dockside. They gave him a resounding thumbs-up in response.

At about a quarter to ten they noticed activity emanating from the far side of Sunderland docks. A large crowd of at least a hundred people was currently marching past the Dockers club. Many of them were brandishing placards and banners bearing slogans demanding workers' rights and strike action. At the head of the crowd 'Red' Len Finch strode purposefully along, followed closely at his heels by his associate Derek Barlow. There was a glint in Mr Finch's eye to suggest he was ready for any kind of stand-off.

He started a chant of 'Strike! Strike!', which was immediately taken up by his supporters.

Bringing up the rear of the column was Labour MP Alan Bailey, who was trailing along disconsolately with a smaller group of his own followers. He could scarcely believe the situation had deteriorated to this level. He was not a happy man.

By ten o'clock the crowd was approaching the quayside where the MS Yellow Rose was moored up. They couldn't believe their eyes when they saw that the cranes were being manned, forklifts were in action and workers were milling around busily checking through their inventories. Senator Earl Sanderson III and his bodyguard had positioned themselves about one third of the way up the freighter's gangway as they watched the work being carried out before them. Alice, Barry and Reggie were standing nonchalantly nearby.

As Len Finch arrived at the scene, he threw a venomous glance towards the hated Tory woman and her lackies, but ultimately he turned his attention to Senator Sanderson.

'Just what do you think you're doing?' he demanded loudly. 'There is a strike in place on these docks! As you full well know!'

Earl turned slowly to face the union boss. Franco followed suit, glaring menacingly.

'*Your* workers may be on strike,' boomed back the senator succinctly. 'But *mine* ain't. As you can see…'

Len Finch could plainly see what was going on. His body was taut with fury.

'What is the meaning of this?' he shouted angrily. The crowd bayed noisily behind him.

'The meaning of this, *comrade*, is that I don't need your workers. The docks are up and running just fine and dandy. Can I do it? *Hell, yeah!*' Earl bawled back. To emphasise the point, he pulled the imitation revolver from its holster and fired off a salvo of loud shots into the air, as was his custom when things were going his way.

The action caused an angry growl to emit from the crowd.

To show his indifference, Earl bellowed '*Yee-haa!*' as vociferously as he could and loosed off another volley of deafening blasts.

*

Chief Immigration Officer Bruce Delaney had been out jogging along the promenade of Roker Beach situated just north of the Sunderland docks. He was coming to the end of his circuit and had stopped for a breather near Sunderland yacht club. He could clearly see the docks across the waters of the River Wear. To his surprise he could hear a great hullabaloo of noise coming from the docklands, as if a huge crowd were gathered making an uproar. As he listened more intently, he could clearly catch the raised voices of men shouting at one another. He was sure one of the voices had an American accent.

Suddenly, in addition to the shouting, there was a series of loud bangs. To Bruce Delaney's trained ear, this was the unmistakable sound of gunfire. For a moment, he shook his head as if his brain couldn't believe what his ears were hearing. But then more gunfire sounded clearly from across the water. And he knew exactly who was responsible. Hellfire, but he'd known those Americans were bad news. He'd confiscated the weapons they'd had on their person when they'd arrived several weeks ago, but they'd obviously had more stashed aboard their freighter. It sounded like a bloody warzone over there.

Reacting instantly, he grabbed his mobile phone from his tracksuit pocket and placed a call to his brother Miles.

Like Bruce, Sergeant Miles Delaney was ex-Forces. He'd been a marksman in the Paras but now worked for Specialist Firearms Command as one of the heads of regional departments. Miles' region covered the North East, and Bruce knew he was currently stationed at Sunderland Police HQ. The call was answered after two rings.

'Bruce! How are you doing?' asked Miles, pleased to be hearing from his brother.

Bruce interrupted him brusquely.

'Miles – listen up. There's no time to explain. There's a serious incident going on in Sunderland docks. There's gunfire involved!'

There was a brief pause while Miles processed the information.

'Okay, roger that. I'll be over with a team in minutes. Can you give me any more info, bro?'

'I don't know much, but some of them are Americans and one of them, a real big bastard, is a trained killer. So be careful!'

'Always am, bro. Thanks. On my way. Over and out.'

The Delaney boys didn't mess about. Bruce knew Miles would have his unit there within five minutes. He wished he could get over there to help, but he was on the wrong side of the river and it'd take him a least twenty minutes to get down to the bridge and back up the other side. It'd be all over by then if Bruce knew his brother. And he knew his brother well.

'I demand you cease working *this instant!*' Len Finch screamed at Senator Sanderson.

Earl pretended to consider the demand. Since his workers were only miming anyway, it was no skin off his nose to cease the charade.

'If I do, will you negotiate this situation reasonably with me?' asked Earl.

Len Finch had little choice but to agree. 'You have my word,' he uttered morosely.

Earl gesticulated to Barry to go and stop the work. Barry went over to the lads holding the clipboards and asked them to hand them in. It was all he could think of on the spur of the moment, but it seemed to satisfy the union boss.

Presently the two leaders, namely Senator Sanderson and Len Finch, finally began to negotiate a settlement. But neither side was willing to concede much, so negotiations were slow.

*

Sergeant Miles Delaney gathered a unit together consisting of two Authorised Firearms Officers equipped with machine guns, another two officers equipped with Tasers, a seasoned Crisis Negotiator and, of course, himself, equipped with a high precision long range sniper rifle. All members of the unit were clad in black overalls with black balaclavas covering their heads. An unmarked police van drove them surreptitiously over the raisable bridge that joined one side of the docks to the other and dropped them out of sight behind some warehouses just south of the main dock.

The unit fanned out around the area and stealthily made its way closer to where the freighter MS Yellow Rose was moored. They then took up a variety of positions to observe the proceedings unfolding before them.

As Miles spied on the scene through his binoculars, all he could see at the moment was a small group of men talking fervently with one another. The larger crowd had temporarily fallen silent, and the workers in the cranes and forklifts had all stopped what they were doing.

As he concentrated his gaze on the two men standing on the gangway, he did observe that the one wearing a black suit was both enormous and ominous. He must be the one Bruce had warned him about. While the one in the cowboy hat did, unbelievably, appear to be casually holding a firearm in his hand. It looked like a revolver.

These boys are a bit tasty, contemplated Miles with some concern.

He continued to monitor the proceedings for a further ten minutes.

*

In the cabin of the gantry crane Kevin was getting hot and bothered. He'd been in the cabin for well over an hour with nothing much happening at all. Below him he could hear people talking and arguing but that was about it. It was getting really boring.

He'd amused himself for the last fifteen minutes by picking his nose and wiping the bogeys on the cabin's

185

windscreen, but even this alluring activity was fast losing its interest.

What was *really* bothering him, though, was that over the course of the last half an hour, his underpants had been slowly riding up between his butt cheeks and were now firmly wedged into the crack of his arse. What's more, due to the cramped conditions in the cabin, he couldn't reach a hand behind his back to pull them back out.

He began fidgeting about awkwardly, which only made matters worse. But then the solution to his predicament suddenly popped into his head. If he could place one hand firmly onto the dashboard and push his arm out, he could then lever himself backwards and arch his back sufficiently so that his other hand could reach round to his backside. *Bonzer!*

He successfully performed the tricky manoeuvre and, to his great relief, managed to fully extricate the offending Y-fronts. He collapsed back into the seat and gave a sigh of intense satisfaction.

Furthermore, as he lifted his hand off the dashboard, he noticed something quite intriguing underneath. There was a large rectangular button. Which was now flashing an amber warning light. The button was marked **Magnet Off**.

Kevin stared at it with morbid curiosity. He wondered if he might have done something a bit foolish. He then heard a mechanism go *Ker-Chunk*. And then he felt a sensation as though a great weight had suddenly been released from the lifting arm of the crane.

Oh, bollocks, he thought.

Released by the magnet, the humongous, heavy container fell through the air like a lugubrious lead brick. It narrowly missed Senator Sanderson and Franco Gambini by a few feet, but did land precisely and squarely on top of the luxurious limousine, Earl III.

The limo was flattened onto the concrete dockside to a thickness of a few inches. It had all but disappeared beneath the container. Only the buffalo horns were left visible, sticking out from under the near end. For several seconds a few bars of the *Star-Spangled Banner* could be heard faintly emanating from the wreckage, but it withered away sadly as the mangled car horn finally gave up the ghost.

Interrupted from his negotiations with the union boss, Earl Sanderson turned to stare agog at the scene that had just transpired before his eyes. He stared in disbelief at the flattened pile of metal that had been his last, cherished, personalised limousine. Disbelief soon turned to anger. He directed his gaze towards the gantry crane where the shocked, gormless face of Kevin could be seen pressed up in horror against the glass window of the cabin door.

'You goddamn, lousy, limey son of a bitch!' he railed up at the hapless Kevin. 'You did that on purpose!'

He lifted his right hand, still grasping the imitation gun, and began firing towards the cabin. He ran out of caps very quickly and had to pause his tirade while he reloaded the gun with fresh ammo. Once he'd finished, he continued firing the gun towards the panic-stricken Kevin.

Kevin had managed to open the cabin window, and began shouting for assistance, unaware that Earl's gun was not real.

'Help!' he cried desperately from the cabin. 'I think he's trying to kill me!'

Kevin tried to open the cabin door to escape, but it was jammed shut and wouldn't budge.

'I'm going to get you, you bastard!' yelled Senator Sanderson, now firing indiscriminately up at the cabin of the crane.

187

Sergeant Miles Delaney had set up his sniper rifle ready for action – just in case – and was watching the scene through the telescopic sight mounted onto the barrel. He'd just observed the driver of the gantry crane try to assassinate the Americans by dropping a container on top of them. They were lucky to have survived. He now witnessed the American wearing the cowboy hat retaliating. He was going berserk and firing his handgun towards the crane driver. His intentions were clearly to kill or maim and Miles had to act quickly.

He rapidly signalled for his team to advance towards the crisis area. They knew what to do and how to handle themselves. The figures in black quickly began to converge towards the crowd of people at the dockside.

Meanwhile, Sergeant Delaney was going to have to deal with the gunman himself. He couldn't allow the man to be firing his handgun around like that. It was a miracle no one had been killed. He'd try to take the gunman out without killing him so he decided to give him a few warning shots. He lined up the crosshairs of his telescopic sight on Earl's Stetson cowboy hat. Just as the American was about to fire his revolver again, Miles pulled the trigger.

*

Still fuming at the destruction of his third and final limousine, Senator Earl Sanderson raised his gun once again. Looking through the sights, he lined up the little spotty punk sat in the crane's cabin and prepared to fire.

'Say your prayers, you little mutha…,' he began.

Suddenly there was the sound of a loud crack and instantaneously Earl's Stetson was blown clean off the top of his head. The bullet had removed the hat with such force that a strong suction effect had taken place, causing the hair on the senator's head to be violently windswept. This had had the unfortunate effect of loosening Earl's toupee from its usual resting place, and it was now sitting up vertically on top of his head looking like a startled hamster.

A second loud crack sounded and the beleaguered toupee was shot off his head altogether and carried right across the docks, where it splattered against the side of the concrete quay and fell lifelessly into the murky waters of the River Wear, never to be seen again.

Earl froze in bewilderment for a moment before finally realising that someone was shooting at him. Someone who was a damn good shot, to boot. He snapped out of it, threw his gun to the ground and dived for cover under the gangway of the MS Yellow Rose. Above him was the hulking form of his black suited bodyguard.

'Franco!' came the senator's orders from below. 'Go get 'em!'

'You got it, boss!' responded the giant figure, stepping down off the gangway and onto the dockside.

Franco Gambini took in the chaotic scene going on around him. People were panicking and running around like headless chickens. It was hard to discern where the enemy was lurking. But he'd heard the shots and seen the accuracy and he knew the opponents he was facing were professionals.

Suddenly, he saw figures in black interspersed with the people in the crowd. The faces were covered in balaclavas.

So, he mused purposefully, *the Triads have finally caught up with us.*

But Franco wasn't afraid of anybody. He'd take out as many of them as he could. Sure, he didn't have his guns, but he was highly proficient in many forms of martial arts and was more than capable of wreaking devastation without them.

Sure enough, one of the figures in black was cautiously approaching him. As it did so, it slowly removed its balaclava and a wizened Asian face smiled knowingly at him. Franco knew the Triad assassins liked to taunt their victims by revealing their identity before a kill. Well, he was going to show this bastard with the grinning face a thing or two.

The face, however, did not belong to a Triad member. It belonged to Crisis Negotiating Officer Ken Li. He was a well-respected veteran who'd learnt his trade with the Hong Kong Police for over twenty years before transferring to the United Kingdom. Officer Li was close to retiring, but still enjoyed his work, especially if he were able to assist with de-escalating a crisis situation.

Ken removed his balaclava as he approached the dangerous looking man with the slicked back hair and black suit. He knew that it was important to deal with situations face to face. He knew too, that it was important to smile and try to diffuse any tension.

He raised his hands, palms open, to show he was no threat. He was about to ask what he could do to help resolve the situation, when to his surprise the big man moved towards him at a speed he didn't believe possible. Before he knew it, his legs had been kicked out from under him and he spun awkwardly in the air before landing in a crumpled heap on the concrete dockside. The impact had dislocated his hip, and he lay inert on the ground, unable to move.

Franco knew he'd taken the man out of action, but now two more figures in black were fast approaching, both armed with machine guns. The first figure raised his weapon at Franco in warning but before he could fire, Franco gave him a vicious karate chop to the neck, accurately hitting the brachial nerve, and stunning the man for a few moments. More than enough time for Franco to punch the second figure in the guts and knee him in the face as he doubled up. Turning his attention back to the figure he'd stunned, he finished him off with a flying kick to the torso.

Within the space of a mere ten seconds, Franco had managed to take down three officers.

*

Alice, Reggie and Barry were watching the carnage ensue all around them with complete shock. They'd never seen anything like it. It had all happened so fast. Reggie was the first to snap out of it. Grabbing Alice's hand, he ushered her over to the minibus, and pulling open the sliding door, they both dived in. They slid the door closed behind them and ducked down behind the seats.

Barry was about to follow them when he became concerned about his good friend Alan Bailey. He knew the Labour MP was a peace-loving man and this outbreak of violence would have appalled him. After a brief search he found him cowering next to one of the fork-lift trucks. He looked terrified. Barry grabbed him by the shoulder of his jacket and heaved him to his feet. They then legged it over to Barry's Montego, got in the front seats and bobbed down below the dashboard. Out of the driver's side window Barry could see the large crowd of panicked people still milling around the dockside. Suddenly he spotted Len Finch and Derek Barlow amongst them. They were desperately trying to get away from the crisis area. Barry saw them shoving their way through the crowd, brutally pushing men, women and the elderly to the ground as they did so. Once through the crowd they pelted it across to the other side of the docks, heading towards the Dockers club and relative safety.

Their actions made Barry sick to his core. But Barry wasn't the only one who'd observed their behaviour. Many of the dockers had witnessed it too and were shaking their fists angrily at the shameless display of the two cowardly union men.

*

Through the telescopic sight of his rifle, Miles Delaney had watched the lethal American bodyguard despatch some of his finest officers. There was nothing Miles could do. He couldn't risk shooting the black suited maniac for fear of hitting innocent bystanders. There were just too many people whizzing around.

He saw his two remaining officers standing close-by. They were armed with the Tasers. Miles signalled to them, in no uncertain terms, to take the big man down forthwith. The two men armed their Tasers and went forward to tackle the crazed bodyguard.

Franco saw them coming, but instead of avoiding them, he actually began to jog towards them in the hope of reaching them before they had the chance to fire. This time, though, he wasn't quite quick enough. The closest officer fired his Taser at Franco. The barbed darts hit him squarely in the chest. The electrodes attached to the darts fizzed with electricity and Franco came to an abrupt halt. The pain to his nervous system was intense, and he felt his body buckle under the strain. But Franco had been trained to endure a lot of pain and he didn't fall.

To Miles Delaney's astonishment, the huge American came back to life, pulled the darts from his chest, and began lumbering towards his officers again. He held his arms straight out in front of him as he stumbled towards them bearing more than a passing resemblance to Frankenstein's monster.

The second officer now raised his Taser to fire. He wasn't sure if anyone could survive being Tasered twice. It'd never happened before. But the huge bodyguard was nearly on top of him and had murder in his eyes. He had to do it.

Just as the officer was about to fire, a few people from the jostling crowd were suddenly pushed towards him and accidentally bumped into his arm. His aim went awry as he fired, and two barbed darts flew from the Taser and embedded themselves into each side of Franco's groin. There was another fizzing of electricity and the bodyguard once again ground to a halt. This time with 1500 volts coursing through his genitals.

Even the mighty Franco couldn't endure this much pain. With a low groan he sank to his knees, toppled over on one side, and finally came to rest flat out on his back. Acrid smoke was pouring from the flies and pockets of his trousers.

The giant bodyguard was finally down, and some calm was returning to the crisis zone.

Senator Earl Sanderson III emerged from his hiding place under the gangway and hurried over to where his stricken colleague lay unconscious on the ground. He fell to his knees, wringing his hands, and remorsefully looked over his fallen companion. He could see that Franco was still breathing but was horribly wounded.

Sergeant Miles Delaney reached the scene with a cry of 'Police! Put your hands up!'

Senator Sanderson turned his head to face him and slowly raised his hands but immediately began bawling at the police officer.

'What in the name of Armstrong's moonboots have you done to him, boy?' Earl demanded, shaking his head sadly.

'We Tasered him,' said Miles weakly.

'You haven't just Tasered him, boy,' Earl berated him. 'You've barbecued his goddamn nuts!'

*

Sergeant Delaney radioed for several ambulances. One for Franco, and the rest for his wounded officers. Once the ambulances had arrived, the officers were driven off rapidly to the A&E department of Sunderland hospital. Franco, however, due to his injuries requiring more specialist care, was blue lighted to the burns unit of the Royal Victoria Infirmary in Newcastle.

Meanwhile, Sergeant Delaney was placing Senator Sanderson under immediate arrest and had handcuffed his hands behind his back. A passing police car had arrived on the scene to assist with the situation and the sergeant was attempting to usher the senator into the back seat. He was not coming quietly.

'Do you know who you're talking to?' Earl hollered at Sergeant Delaney. 'I am none other than Senator Earl Sanderson III! Of Texas!'

'Yes,' replied Miles unperturbed. 'And I could hear you if you were in Texas, too!'

Miles grabbed an arm and tried to physically shove him in the car.

'Get your hands off me, boy!' Earl lambasted him. 'What are you arresting me for, anyway, goddammit? You saw that my associate and I were being attacked by those hoodlums!'

'Those *hoodlums* happened to be police officers. Some of my finest men!' snarled back Miles in reply. 'Officer Li may never walk again after what your psychotic bodyguard did to him.'

Realisation was starting to dawn on the American. He could well be in big trouble. He looked around for Alice, in the hope that she might be able to help him out again. But the area had been cordoned off, and Alice, Barry, Reggie and Alan could only look on helplessly from a distance. There was only one thing that occurred to the senator to do in a situation like this. And that was to shout some more.

As he began roaring and railing at the police again, Sergeant Delaney had had enough. He put his hand on the now bald dome of Earl's head and shoved him down firmly and roughly into the back seat of the car.

'All right, Senator,' he said, deliberately patting his bald spot. 'Keep your hair on!'

On that final humiliating note, the police car drove Earl away, taking with it any hope he may have had of his plans succeeding. He had singularly and spectacularly failed in returning the docks to productivity.

15.

As soon as Alice had got back to her flat, she'd telephoned her father at Chesham Manor. After explaining exactly what had happened, she beseeched him to call the Chancellor of the Duchy of Lancaster and try and get him to contact the Home Secretary for his assistance once again. Humphrey had told her he'd do his best.

Twenty-four hours later, and after a night in the cells, an official pardon had been granted by the Home Office for Senator Sanderson. His bodyguard, Franco Gambini, despite hospitalising three police officers, had also been exonerated from any blame. The whole incident had been brushed off as being a huge misunderstanding, and that the Americans were simply defending themselves. It had not been fully established exactly how the shipping container had come to crash down onto the limousine. When the operator of the crane, Mr Kevin Butterworth, had been interviewed by the police, he had bizarrely attempted to blame the whole catastrophe on his underpants. The police psychologist had thought the poor lad was suffering with post-traumatic stress disorder and had sent him off for counselling.

It had been discovered that the senator's firearm was merely a child's cap gun and that he'd been using it only as a prop in line with his American cowboy persona. Frankly, according to the Home Office, the police should have known better. Both the Delaney brothers had been given serious reprimands for their overzealous policing. They were to consider themselves fortunate that all the officers who had been injured in the line of duty were predicted to make a full recovery.

*

Franco had received specialist treatment from the surgeons at the Royal Victoria Infirmary's burns unit. It was going to take him many weeks to fully recover, but the doctors were confident that there would only be minor scarring caused by the electrical burns to his groin. Unfortunately, they had not been able to resuscitate his frazzled testicles, and he'd been given the sad news that he was never likely to have children. Not that this bothered Franco in the slightest. He'd never had himself down as a family man anyway.

Alice had driven Senator Sanderson up to visit him in hospital. When Earl saw that Franco was on an open ward he immediately paid for him to be placed in a private room. He wanted only the best for his loyal bodyguard. The two men had talked at length and Franco had assured his boss that he'd be back to work just as soon as he was discharged from hospital.

*

As soon as Baroness Billingbrooke had heard about the incident, she'd called the senator on his mobile phone. Earl filled her in on the whole story and told her about Franco's injuries. He explained that it would be some weeks before he was fully recovered.

Harriet had immediately insisted that, while Franco was convalescing, Earl should stay with her at her estate near Cromer. She instructed him to pack a bag and be ready for her arrival in a few hours' time. She was going to drive up in her Lotus straight away. The senator couldn't agree fast enough. The thought of seeing her again, and actually staying with her, filled him with giddy excitement. She would be the perfect remedy for his woes. The drive would take Harriet about five hours. Earl used the time to pack his things and tidy up his affairs. This would include a monumentally important phone call to Alice Chesham.

Alice had been expecting a call from the senator, to be honest. But the significance of what transpired in the call took her completely by surprise. Earl had begun by thanking her and her father once again for their assistance with the Home Office and getting him out of trouble. He then informed her he would be moving in with her Aunt Harri for the foreseeable future, which had caused Alice to raise an eyebrow. Knowing her aunt well, she'd considered whether she should warn Earl about her aunt's wilder side. But then thought it'd be better if Earl found out for himself.

But the big bombshell was that Earl was passing full responsibility of dealing with the situation in Sunderland docks entirely to Alice. He admitted his own failure in the matter. His blunt but sincere honesty impressed her. He was going to give her full rein to do whatever she deemed necessary to achieve their objectives. Money would be no object. He would back her to the hilt. His only requirement was that she keep him fully in the loop of what was going on. But he assured her he would not interfere with or question her decisions.

Alice had been totally dumbfounded for a few moments. But she was made of stern stuff, and of course, she accepted the gauntlet and rose to the challenge. She thanked the senator profusely for putting his trust in her abilities. The telephone conversation was concluded and they hung up.

She couldn't wait to tell Barry and Reggie the news.

*

Reggie was busy restocking the bar at the Dockers club. Ever since the club had been refurbished, more and more customers had come drifting through the doors. Reggie had noticed that there was a definite uptick of women now coming in, in particular. Alice certainly came in most evenings to spend time with him, chatting over the bar. Grandma Lilly would often come in and join them too. He'd also contacted many of his friends who were musicians or in bands and encouraged them to come and play. The place was getting a reputation as a cool live music venue. The dockers, especially, were pleased as punch about their new establishment. Reggie did his best to subtly remind them where the money had come from. It was slowly being acknowledged.

Reggie had just finished putting the remaining bottles in the chiller when Alice and Barry burst into the bar in a state of high excitement.

Alice flew across the barroom and hugged and kissed Reggie hotly.

'Wow! What was that for?' he asked with curious surprise.

In a breathless flurry of words Alice told him of her news that Earl was entrusting her completely with the situation in the docks. When she'd finished, she stood staring at him in feverish anticipation. Reggie smiled warmly, congratulated her, and then hugged and kissed her lovingly in response.

'I've got some great ideas that we can start putting into place,' said Alice enthusiastically. 'I'm going to make it impossible for that Len Finch to keep on striking.'

'You go, girl!' said Reggie supportively.

'Aye,' added Barry. 'And he'll be keepin' his heed doon at the moment, anyway. What wi' the union leader elections cummin' up, an all that.'

199

Alice and Reggie both did a double take and turned in unison to goggle at Barry.

'Did you just say *union leader elections*, Barry?' asked Alice with intent.

'Oh, aye, lass. They happen every five years or so, I reckon,' he replied. 'Why do ye ask?'

'Don't you see, Barry?' Alice explained. 'This is our chance to get 'Red' Len out of office! We'd just need someone to run against him.'

'Oh, nar, nar. Ye've nay chance of that pet,' said Barry vehemently. 'No one would dare gan up against 'im. Ye'd have to be two cups short o' a tea set.'

Alice caught Reggie's eye and they both exchanged a hidden look of mutual understanding. She gave him a crafty wink.

'What we'd need,' considered Reggie, rubbing his chin, 'is someone with real experience of working the docks.'

'Someone who knows how to work all the machinery, you mean?' added Alice.

'Yes,' continued Reggie. 'Preferably someone who's even had a supervisory role.'

'Yes,' chimed Alice. 'Of course, he'd also have to be well liked and respected by the other dockers.'

'Absolutely,' concurred Reggie. 'And naturally he'd have to know all about the processes, paperwork and administration too.'

'He'd have to be a special kind of man,' said Alice fervently. 'A man with passion, pride and integrity, and a willingness to face adversity for the sake of the common good.'

200

Alice and Reggie looked to Barry as if for confirmation.

'Aye, nay doubt aboot it,' Barry agreed, nodding his head. 'But where on earth will we find a sucker like that, eh?'

Alice and Reggie said nothing more, but both were smiling sweetly at Barry, who was smiling innocently back. Slowly but surely, however, the smile slipped from Barry's face as he realised the intentions of his two colleagues.

'Aw, bugger,' he said.

*

Harriet's yellow Lotus zoomed through the Sunderland docklands and pulled up alongside the MS Yellow Rose around mid-afternoon. She pipped the horn to let Earl know she'd arrived. Almost immediately Senator Sanderson appeared on the gangway, complete with a small suitcase. He was all ready to go.

As he walked down the gangway, Harriet noticed something different about him. It wasn't so much that he wasn't wearing his trademark Stetson. It was more that he was now exhibiting quite a pronounced bald spot. *We'll have to be doing something about that*, she mused, as he approached the sports car. But she was pleased the toupee was gone, at any rate.

She alighted from the car as he approached and she flung herself into his arms and kissed him passionately full on the mouth.

'Howdy, Harri,' he managed to say, once they'd come up for air.

'Good afternoon,' she smiled. 'It was quite a long trip up here, Earl. Would you be a sweetheart and drive us back?'

'Er,' he mumbled.

'Don't worry. You're fully insured. I rang my broker and saw to that on the way up.'

'Well, gee. If you're sure, I'd be happy to oblige.'

'I'm quite sure,' she confirmed.

Earl slung his suitcase in the tiny boot and then settled himself in the driver's seat. Harriet made herself comfortable on the passenger side. Earl had never driven such a small sports car before, but as he pulled away from the docks and headed out onto the main roads, he was thoroughly enjoying the thrill of driving the nifty Lotus. He was sure going to relish the drive back to Norfolk.

'Now, you crazy Brits drive on the wrong side of the road,' he declared as they shot off down the dual carriageway. 'So, you just make sure I don't stray on the wrong side, y'hear?'

'Actually,' she informed him, 'we British drive on the correct side of the road, and it is you colonialists that have it all wrong. And don't worry about straying. You won't be doing that while I'm around.'

She left the statement hanging ambiguously in the air, but observing her in the driver's mirror, Earl noticed she was trying to conceal a wicked smile.

Damn, but he loved this dame.

It had gone past ten o'clock by the time they reached the entrance to the Billingbrooke Estate. They'd stopped en route to give Earl a break from driving and to grab a bite to eat. They hadn't made bad time at all. Earl drove the car down the sweeping gravelled drive that was almost half a mile long. He eventually pulled up onto the huge ornate drive of

Billingbrooke Hall. The Hall was gothic in style and resembled a small castle. It had touches of a French château with its many spiral turrets.

Earl fished his suitcase out of the Lotus' boot while Harriet went up the stone steps of the grand entrance portico to open the enormous oak wooden front door. All the staff had clocked off for the night so they were all alone. They entered the hall and stood for a moment in the huge, magnificent entrance hall. An impressive galleried staircase led up to the upper floors. Harriet's pussycat, Galore, appeared out of the darkness and began to entwine herself around Harriet's ankles, as cats do. Harriet gave her a fuss and then shooed her away.

'Well, it's been a long day,' murmured Harriet. 'I suggest we turn in. I'll show you around the place tomorrow if that's all right with you.'

'Sure thing,' replied Earl. 'I'm pretty beat myself.'

Taking Earl by the hand she led him up the wide galleried stairway and up to the next floor. But they didn't stop here. Instead, she led him up the stairs again to the second floor.

'I like a good view from my bedroom,' she said by way of explanation.

Baroness Billingbrooke's bedroom consisted of a suite of rooms which took up nearly half of the whole second floor. Her rooms were made up of her bedroom, featuring a king-size four poster bed, a large dressing room, two cavernous walk-in wardrobes and an en suite that had a gigantic sunken whirlpool bath as its centrepiece.

'Welcome to my little boudoir,' she smirked saucily as she led Earl through the door.

He'd barely made it over the threshold when Harriet launched herself at him. She began tearing off his clothes with the frenzied passion of a wild tigress. Senator Earl Sanderson

III stood stunned for a moment. No woman had ever been quite like this with him before. But he soon snapped out of it, tossed the suitcase he was still clutching to one side, and began frantically undressing Harriet in turn.

Harriet jumped into his arms and wrapped her legs around his waist to cling on to him. Kissing each other passionately all the while, Earl carried her towards the four-poster bed where they fell lustily onto the sheets in a tangle of arms and legs. Earl paused for a moment while he gazed adoringly into Harriet's eyes. She gazed back at him and licked her lips with the tip of her tongue raunchily.

'Well, what are you waiting for?' she breathed in his ear. 'Ride 'em, cowboy!'

If anyone had been passing through the grounds of the Billingbrooke Estate that night, the peaceful and serene atmosphere would have been rudely shattered by the loud and boisterous hollering of a Texan man shouting '*Yee-haa!*' at the top of his voice.

*

Now that Alice had been given free rein, she began to put her plans into action. Borrowing from her environmental proposals from her time as MP for North Norfolk, she made it a policy of her manifesto that Sunderland docks, with the full backing of Lone Star Freight, were to be as ecologically friendly as possible. The docks machinery was to be either converted to run on green, unpolluting fuels or, wherever possible, to run with electricity. She'd sent the proposals through to Senator Sanderson in an emailed communique. He'd green-lighted the proposals so fast, she'd wondered if he'd actually read them. For some reason, his mind seemed to be focused elsewhere.

Her ambitious plans for the future included getting Earl to convert his vast fleet of freighters to use biodiesel, liquefied natural gas, or even an electric hybrid. She knew that was a big ask, but she fully intended having her Aunt Harri on board, and she had a sneaky feeling that Harriet would easily be able to twist the senator's arm (amongst other things). Anyway, whatever concessions she got out of Senator Sanderson would all bode well for her political career.

Humphrey and Henrietta had invited Alice, Reggie and Barry down to Chesham Manor for a few days over the weekend. Humphrey, with Carstairs' assistance, was desperate to help out in any way he could. Alice had explained her plan of putting Barry up as a contender for the next union boss. Although Barry was very knowledgeable about working the docks and the role that the union played in the trade, he was hopeless at writing and making speeches. Humphrey and Carstairs immediately offered their support. Humphrey promised Barry that before they all returned to Sunderland, he would be armed with a top-notch speech to deliver when the elections were held. They were also going to instruct him in the art of oration. Combined with Barry's affable personality and people skills, they believed he had an excellent chance of knocking 'Red' Len off his perch. Barry was made up.

Alfie, too, had expressed an interest in joining in with their plans. He was hoping he might pick up a few tips for his own career. He was especially keen to learn of Alice's environmental ideas. He'd known she'd started putting her proposals into action whilst she was still MP for North Norfolk. Alfie really wanted to carry on her good work. Of course, Alice was only too happy to help out her little brother and the two of them had spent hours discussing the subject. Although Alfie was not the quickest student, by the time Alice had finished lecturing him, he had a comprehensive knowledge of a wide range of environmental initiatives.

Alice and Reggie had taken the opportunity of the visit to announce that they were officially a couple. Reggie would be moving out of his Grandma Lilly's house and into

Alice's flat as soon as they got back. The announcement had been met with much pleasure from the Chesham household. Everyone was very fond of Reggie, and they'd never seen Alice so happy in a relationship.

There had been only one hiccup over the weekend regarding interfamily relations. It had involved Henrietta (of course) making a comment over dinner about the length of Reggie's hair. She'd gone on to enquire as to when he intended to have a proper haircut. Reggie had responded by informing her that his dreadlocks were like a part of his soul, and that under no circumstances was he considering removing them. He went on to advocate that perhaps people should adopt the adage of 'live and let live'.

To lead by example, he'd informed her that he very much admired the beginnings of the moustache that she was growing, and that he thought it looked very distinguished.

There were indeed some errant hairs, that in Henrietta's older age, had begun to sprout from her top lip. She didn't think anyone had noticed. Her initial reaction to Reggie's comments was that her features seemed to develop severe frostbite. Everyone else around the table also froze in shock at his daring reply. Except Alfie who couldn't help snickering. But slowly and steadily the icy demeanour began to melt away from her face as she realised the lad had totally outfoxed her. She even began to laugh. She liked a man with spirit, and he'd certainly shown some backbone. In her estimation, Reggie had just climbed even higher than ever.

Reggie had breathed a sigh of relief, as had Alice.

*

Franco was recovering well at the Royal Victoria Infirmary in Newcastle. After a week he'd been able to take his first steps. It was predicted that in another few weeks he'd be back walking normally again. The senator kept in regular contact with him and made sure he was comfortable.

*

Earl and Harriet had spent the last fortnight in a blur of sightseeing, wining and dining, horse riding, shooting, and, of course, lots of raw and passionate love making. Harriet liked to take the lead in that department, which suited Earl just fine. She clearly had a lot more experience in the matter than he did. He never knew what kinky escapade she was going to come up with next. Little did Earl know she was only just getting started. The two were head over heels in love with each other. They'd both found their soulmate.

Following the loss of his hairpiece, Harriet had taken him into a barber shop in Cromer and given strict instruction that he was to have his hair cropped very short. She'd told him he must embrace his baldness, not hide it. It was a sign of virility, she'd told him. She'd certainly tested the theory at any rate. And she hadn't been disappointed.

Alice, Barry and Reggie had kept in touch and provided the senator with daily updates as to what was transpiring up in Sunderland. The trade union leader elections were only a day or so away. Alice had invited Earl and Harriet to attend, along with Humphrey, Henrietta, Carstairs and Alfie. It was promising to be a proper battle, and Alice wanted as much support for Barry as possible.

16.

At 9:30 on the morning of the election day, Len Finch was sat, as usual, at his desk in his office in central Sunderland. He was feeling supremely confident. He knew very well that the pathetic Tory woman had put up her lackey, Barry Higgins, to stand against him. He'd no doubt that she'd had to bribe him to do so. That's how the capitalist pigs worked. And he knew too that the little worm Higgins would have taken the money. But that's why they were going to lose.

No one had a purer heart that Leonard Finch. Money or material possessions did not interest him. He knew only Marxist doctrine and socialist principles were what were important at the end of the day. That's what the workers wanted, and that's why they'd vote for him. And he had no intention of letting them down. The billionaire Sanderson would be facing strikes and protests for years to come. Len allowed himself a rare smile.

The door to his office opened and Derek Barlow's grim features appeared around the door frame.

'Are you ready to leave?' he asked bluntly. 'We need to be in the docks by 10am.'

'I'm aware of that, brother,' replied Len calmly. 'I am ready to perform my solemn duty.'

As he rose importantly from his desk and gathered his papers to leave, Derek Barlow raised his eyes to the ceiling and tutted under his breath.

They made their way over to the docks in good time. A large crowd of dock workers were already in attendance. The Labour MP Alan Bailey and his supporters were amongst them. Len noted that Barry Higgins was also there, along with Alice Chesham, Senator Sanderson and a whole host of their fascist associates.

The union leader vote was a simple affair. The two contenders would give their speeches and, when completed, the vote would take place then and there, right on the dockside. Once all the ballot papers had been counted by an independent official, the next leader of the union would be announced.

Mr Len Finch was invited to make his speech first. True to form, it consisted of his tried and tested spiel about his comrades, workers, brothers and sisters standing in solidarity against the exploitation and greed perpetrated by the right-wing scum. No attempt was to be made to negotiate a settlement. There was to be no end to the strike action whilst he was the union boss.

His speech received a resounding cheer and rowdy applause from many of the dockers and his loyal supporters. Len joined his hands above his head and punched the air in triumph. He was sure he had this in the bag.

Mr Barry Higgins was then invited to make his speech. There were some boos before he'd even started. Barry looked extremely ill at ease. Nerves were clearly getting to him. Len Finch was mocking him for his lack of confidence.

Barry started his speech regardless. He began by explaining how he was a simple local man, who had no serious knowledge of political factions. Barry told the crowd that he had worked on the docks most of his adult life. He'd earned a reasonable wage, and he'd been grateful for the money and the chance to support himself and enjoy a simple but satisfying life. He'd known the previous owners of the docks had struggled to keep it running. They'd had no money for re-investment or new infrastructure. They'd had to lay off many workers. Barry himself had been made redundant. He'd been inconsolable with despair. He'd had to take any job that came his way. Despite being a lifelong Labour voter, he'd accepted a job offer from Mr Giles Wight to work as his secretary for the Tory Party. (Alice hadn't known this and now raised an eyebrow in surprise.) He wasn't ashamed of it, he stated, because he'd needed a job. And to be fair to his employer, Mr. Wright had been a decent and honourable man. The docks now had a new owner, Barry continued, who was a powerful and successful American named Senator Sanderson. The senator wanted the docks to thrive, and he had the money to invest. Barry described how he had gotten to know him over the past months. Sure, there were differences of opinion, and the senator wasn't perfect, but Barry thought that underneath all the bravado and show, there lay a man who could be trusted. In conclusion, therefore, a vote for Barry Higgins would be a vote to return to work. It would be a vote for a re-negotiated and improved work contract. It would be a vote for supporting better working conditions. It'd be a vote for investing in the docks, the workers, and their future. It'd be a vote for common sense.

For a moment, there was only a stunned silence. Barry looked up from his speech notes apprehensively. A single person began to clap. Then there were two. Then three. And then many dozens of people in the crowd were clapping and cheering him along. Barry had prevailed.

Len Finch looked on furiously. *How could the stupid masses believe such lies?* He scowled bad temperedly.

The dockers were now lining up to vote. There was just a trestle table set up on the dockside, upon which was placed the ballot box. The adjudicator was sat on a chair behind the table, closely monitoring the proceedings. Everyone eligible was holding an official ballot paper. The votes began to be cast and were going rapidly into the ballot box. Half an hour later, all the votes were in.

The independent adjudicator then opened the ballot box and began the count. The crowd knew it wouldn't take long before the result was announced. Some of Mr Finch's supporters hoisted Len up onto their shoulders ready for the celebratory victory parade.

Barry waited anxiously and began to fidget about. Alice went over to him and kissed him gently on his cheek.

'Whatever happens,' she told him sincerely, 'I want you to know that I am so very proud of you.'

Barry smiled at her and wiped a tear from his eye. 'But I'm not even a bloomin' Tory, pet.'

'That's not important, Barry,' she said with feeling. 'I still think you're amazing, whatever your views!'

Alice stood by his side while they waited for the result to come in. Alan Bailey MP came over to congratulate him on his speech and stood steadfastly on his other side.

The result was in. The adjudicator cleared her voice to announce the winner.

'Mr Len Finch,' she proclaimed. 'One hundred and twenty-seven votes.'

A tumultuous cheer rose up from the crowd as Len was lifted from his supporters' shoulders and into the air. Len was grinning madly and waving his hands frantically at the crowd.

'Mr Barry Higgins,' interrupted the adjudicator as silence fell on the crowd. 'One hundred and forty-two votes.'

An even louder cheer erupted from the crowd as deafening applause, whistling and excited hollering filled the air. Barry was just looking around completely dumbstruck.

'I hereby declare the new leader of the union to be,' continued the adjudicator, 'Mr Barry Higgins.'

Barry was beaming from ear to ear. He'd actually done it! Humphrey, Henrietta, Alfie and Carstairs were applauding even louder than everyone else and congratulating Barry heartily on his win.

A huge crowd of Barry's supporters suddenly swept across the quayside towards Len's supporters and lifted the stricken Mr Finch from their shoulders and onto their own. For a moment Len believed the adjudicator had made some sort of mistake, and the supporters were protesting the result by hoisting him onto their own shoulders. But he was wrong.

With a mighty combined heave, 'Red' Len was launched into the air on a trajectory very much aimed at flying over the quayside and into the murky brown waters of the River Wear. With a terrible, high-pitched scream, Len plummeted fifteen feet down, and belly flopped gracelessly into the turbid waters of the dock. He was accompanied by a large jeering cheer.

Derek Barlow, having witnessed his boss taking a plunge, tentatively leaned over the quayside to see if he was all right. Just behind him, Mr Alan Bailey MP, was walking nonchalantly by. As he did so, Mr Barlow mysteriously lost his balance and went nose-first into an untidy dive straight into the water next to his master.

'Goodness me,' proclaimed the Labour MP innocently. 'However did *that* happen?'

Alice and Reggie, who had been watching the scene with interest, had noticed the almost indiscernible shove. They burst out laughing and gave him a great round of applause. Mr Bailey, feigning shock, protested his innocence vehemently. But not for very long.

Meanwhile, the crowd had now hoisted Barry up onto their shoulders and were parading him around the docks in a victory march. Barry was loving it. He still couldn't believe he'd won.

Senator Sanderson, taking in the scene, remained silent for once. He gave Baroness Billingbrooke a polite hug. It was his only sign of emotion. Harriet had been firmly instructing him on how to conduct himself more cordially whilst in polite society. For a start she'd confiscated his toy handgun. That bloody thing had caused more than enough trouble.

The senator remained calm and demure, as instructed.

Inside, of course, he was jumping for joy. He led Harriet sedately up the gangway of the MS Yellow Rose, where they were residing whilst in Sunderland. They waved graciously to the crowd, who gave them a hearty cheer, and then retired discreetly inside. He showed her through to his private staterooms, where they settled on the sofa in the comfortable lounge area and opened a celebratory bottle of champagne. His sleeping quarters were located just off the lounge, and the vast cabin contained an emperor size bed made up with purple and crimson satin sheets. Baroness Billingbrooke, thoroughly approving of the glamorous bedroom, began making sordid plans for further celebrations later on.

*

Over the course of the following weeks, things moved very quickly. With Barry now in charge of the union, the dockers had a representative working *genuinely* on behalf of their best interests. A deal was speedily thrashed out with the boss of Lone Star Freight to get them all back to work. It hadn't been particularly difficult. Essentially, Senator Sanderson had ended up giving Barry anything he asked for. Even when Earl didn't agree with something, Alice had simply to make a surreptitious phone call to her Aunt Harri and suddenly he would change his mind. Alice wasn't entirely

213

sure how her aunt performed the trick and, frankly, she didn't want to know. But it was a very efficient system.

For starters, all the workers were to retain their jobs. There would be no layoffs. On top of that, all the dockers were to receive a ten per cent pay rise, they were to get an extra day off every year, and they were to get better working conditions, sick pay and overtime. Also, and possibly most popular of all, a pool table was to be installed in the back room of the newly refurbished Dockers club.

Over time, more investment would be made into Sunderland docks, including new environmentally friendly machinery (as per Alice's initiatives), and the MS Yellow Rose would be the first freighter of Earl's fleet to be converted to run on liquefied natural gas. It was an exciting time for the docks.

It was good news politically too. Naturally, with Earl's blessing, Alice had made sure her name and face had been splashed all over the newspapers as the main backer of Lone Star Freight's successful takeover and transformation of the docks.

*

Franco had now made a full recovery from his injuries and was expressing a desire to return home to Texas. Earl had listened to his request and agreed to fly him back to Houston on the next available first-class ticket.

As a trusted associate, the senator had given his loyal bodyguard, Mr Gambini, clear instructions to run the business back in Houston in his absence. However, Franco was to collaborate closely with his secretary Lorna Wheeler, who knew the day-to-day dealings of the company inside out. They were both to report back to him regularly.

214

In the meantime, Earl had decided to remain in England to get a really good grip on his own affairs. As it were.

*

With the docks up and running and the trade union now playing ball, Alice could finally concentrate more on her own political career. Of course, all the good work with the docks would help, but now she could begin tackling other environmental and ecological issues that were close to her heart. Not to mention a whole range of other issues important in the Sunderland area. Reggie had been hugely instrumental in helping her identify these more local needs.

Reggie had also been doing his best to improve her image following her drunken ramblings at the last political speech day. Most folk now knew the truth of what had happened that day. All of them had been appalled at what Derek Barlow had done. There was even a rumour that the ex-union boss, Len Finch, had been involved.

All of which was now academic, as both men had completely disappeared off the face of the earth. No one missed them.

All too soon, the General Election was fast approaching. The election date had been set to be held on 4th July.

Alice was determined to do her very best.

As the whole country became transfixed with the world of politics, no longer was she known as *Alice in Norfolk*.

She was most definitely *Alice in Sunderland*.

When the election had finally come around, she'd worked her socks off to get the best possible outcome for her political party. It had been a Herculean task.

Epilogue

In the General Election of 2024, the Conservative Party were roundly and steadfastly defeated. In fact, the Tories took a trouncing unlike anything they'd ever encountered in their entire history, managing to take only 23.7% of the vote. It was an unmitigated disaster.

The reason for their demise was entirely down to their own gross incompetence, deep-rooted corruption, and never-ending scandals.

However, there was one place in the United Kingdom where there was a little blip that bucked the trend. And that place was Sunderland. The General Election results were as follows:

Labour (hold)	Alan Bailey	18,567	Share Change -3%
Conservative	Alice Chesham	9,798	Share Change +16%
Lib Dem	Neil Price	4,167	Share Change -2%
Green	Rebecca Davis	2,643	Share Change -3%
Others	Various	2,321	Share Change -8%

*

The re-elected Labour MP for Sunderland, Alan Bailey, was interviewed shortly after his unanimous victory.

Despite losing a small percentage of his own vote, he was quoted as saying that he was not at all bitter. In fact, he rather admired the up-and-coming Conservative politician, Alice Chesham, and he was greatly impressed with her good work in the docklands.

*

Former docker Barry Higgins went on to become one of the most popular leaders the trade union had ever had. He became known as the very epitome of a man of the people.

*

Alfred Chesham, MP for North Norfolk, had managed to hang on to his seat. This was largely put down to his being regarded as a well-respected and impeccably presented pillar of the community. With his extensive knowledge of offshore tax havens and environmental reforms, he was now considered a very safe pair of hands.

Alfie continued to reside at Chesham Manor with his proud parents, Lord Humphrey and Lady Henrietta Chesham. His unofficial mentor, the magnificent Carstairs, was prouder still.

*

The front page of the prestigious *Norfolk Style* magazine had announced the engagement of Baroness Harriet

Billingbrooke to American tycoon Senator Sanderson. It was going to be the wedding of the year.

The magazine could exclusively reveal that, once married, the senator was going to adopt the title:

Baron Earl Sanderson III of Billingbrooke and Texas.

Which, frankly, was going to confuse the hell out of everybody.

*

The former Chancellor of the Duchy of Lancaster had been extremely pleased and impressed with Alice's performance in the General Election. So much so, that he had written a letter to her to congratulate her and to offer her the next available safe seat that came up for grabs in the Tory Party.

Alice had replied to thank the chancellor but had politely declined his offer. She'd expressed her sincere desire to continue to live and work exactly where she was.

You see, not only had she fallen madly in love with a rather special man called Reggie, but she'd also fallen in love with the characterful people, the colourful culture and the wholly wonderful place known as Sunderland.

Acknowledgements

I'd like to thank my wife Lois Capsticks for her unerring support, Lucy Spink for editing, TJ Mudadi-Billings for assistance with the cover design, Richard Ngwa for advice, and Marisha Curry for proof reading. Thank you!

Printed in Dunstable, United Kingdom